The Apocalypse of Enoch

Desolation

An End of Days Novel

Shane Moore

Names, characters, places, and incidents either are the product of the author's imagination or are used fictitiously. Any resemblance to actual persons, living or dead, events, or locales is entirely coincidental.

This work, including all characters, names, and places: Copyright 2015 Shane Moore, unless otherwise noted.

Cover art and interior design by Kendall R. Hart. Character likenesses used with permission from Shane Moore.

No part of this book may be reproduced or transmitted in any form or by any means, electronic or mechanical, including photocopying, recording, or by any information storage and retrieval system, without the written permission of both the publisher and author.

All rights reserved.

A New Babel Book release
381 High Point Drive
Holiday Shores, IL 62025

www.newbabelbooks.com

ISBN 978-1-63196-010-9 (trade paperback)
First printing.

Printed in the United States of America.

Acknowledgments

I want to thank my friend, Kendall R. Hart and his Grimstone studios, for all the talent and time that goes into bringing the world in my mind to reality, be that paper, clay, or pixel.

"The Nephilim were on the earth in those days, and also afterward, when the sons of God came in to the daughters of man and they bore children to them."

Genesis 6:4

1
DAYS OF SEVEN

The sun rose high above the eastern horizon and started to bake the dry Texas ground.

April walked on the side of the road. She was thirsty, but was rationing her water. She had a sea bag she snagged from the ship with spare clothes, some food, and basic utensils. She didn't know how long she would have before the sickness overtook her.

The hot sun cooked the asphalt. She had to walk on the side of the road in the dirt to keep from burning her feet. Sweat beaded up on her smooth caramel skin. April walked for most of the morning and came up on a small town. Debris and metal were all over the road and seemed to stretch for miles. Large corrugated steel from barn roofs were scattered into the field. She could see some mobile homes were on their sides and a four way red light that hung across the road was lying on the street. The power had long been out so she didn't worry about the downed lines. The city limit sign had been ripped from the post and laid on another pile of tin. She could barely make out the name; "Arroyo Colorado Estates."

April started towards the pile of debris. She could hear something small growling and whimpering under it. Reaching down slowly, April drew her pistol and lifted it the thin metal sign. Her eyes feasted on horror. A feral child was hiding under the tin. He was wearing a small black t-shirt with blue and orange logo that said "Vorto." His skin was gray, like the others, but he was not muscular. His light colored hair was long and stringy, and his big green eyes stared back at her while his mouth offered a large yellow toothed grin. The little monster held a dead armadillo in his hand and he crunched and chewed the hard scales. April raised her pistol and pointed it at the little beast's head. The feral boy smiled as he chewed and turned his head to the side. April's finger slid from the guard to the trigger. She squinted one eye and began to squeeze.

The boy smiled through his chewing and held up the dead carcass, offering it to her. Its tender intestines spilled out and fell onto the hot dirt. He made whimpering sounds and motioned for her to take it.

April shook her head and let the tin fall back down. "Damn," she muttered. April holstered her pistol and started walking further down the road. To her left was an overgrown field, and to her right was the small town. She could hear an odd scraping sound behind her. She turned to see the feral had made it out from under the tin and was starting towards her in the street. The little monster did not have any legs. They were missing at his hips and he sat in the center of a bright red push mower that was missing the engine. He was strapped in with an odd harness. He pulled himself forward with one hand and clutched the rotting armadillo carcass in the other. April lifted her gun and pointed it at the little beast. "Get the hell away from me!"

The monster paused and cocked its head to the side to try and figure out what she was communicating. April turned back and stared down the road. Her mind wandered back to the ship. How had she gotten infected? Randy had been bit by the spider. Jeff—the monkey. Corey was bit when she met him. But, how had every kid changed? She had not seen a single child under age thirteen, and she knew from the last day that reports were every child in the Saint Louis metro area had fallen ill. And why did Corey turn into a giant rager in a matter of hours and Jeff took months and was smaller and laughed a lot?

April's thoughts were roused by a calloused, rough skinned hand that intertwined it's little fingers into hers. The hand was burning hot to the touch. She jerked it free and raised her pistol. "Get the hell away from me!"

The little beasts looked at her confused. Tears welled up in its big childlike eyes and dripped down its crusted face. *Was this thing crying?* April's thoughts drifted back to the rager that burst into the KTVI building in Saint Louis. She thought it looked like her friend Tim. It didn't attack her. Did these things have some humanity left that she didn't know of?

April felt dizzy. She wiped sweat from her forehead and started back down the road. She could hear the little zombie boy squeaking and dragging behind her. She kept walking until she came up to a four way. She paused for several minutes struggling with which way to go. To her right and the left, the road was narrower and not lined. April felt the tiny hand grab hers again. She looked down. The little beast smiled with a childlike innocence. He looked up at her with sad eyes. April smiled haphazardly. He didn't seem threatening and scary like the others. To her surprise, he smiled back and then looked straight ahead. His watery eyes gazed out at the horizon, trying to see what April was looking at.

"So, what's your name?"

The boy didn't look up. He just stared down the road.

"It says Vorto on your shirt. How about I call you that?"

The monster readjusted his grip on her hand.

April smiled, "Vorto it is."

She walked straight through the intersection. Vorto scooted along the ground with his free hand to keep up with her.

The hot Texas sun pounded down on the dark asphalt of the old country road. Small bits of tar and oil bubbled up and popped when Kurt and Andy's bicycle tires rode over them. Kurt stood up in the peddles and pushed his way up the hill.

He had to be careful not to have his prosthetic leg slip off.

Kurt glanced back at his brother. Andy had got off and was push walking his bike up the rest of the hill.

"Come on, pussy. This is a small one." Andy waved his hand in dismissal and wiped the sweat from his brow. Kurt chuckled to himself and crested the small Texan hill. In the distance he could see a two pump run-down gas station. The windows were boarded up and it looked like there was something stored on the roof. He scanned from north to south to see if he could spy any danger, but he saw nothing. Andy slowly rode up beside him. Sweat trickled down his brow and off of his chin. "Fuck this heat, man."

"We need water. See that service station? Looks like someone's living there."

Andy wiped his face with his shirt. "Yeah, but it's not like we have anything to trade. And the way things are now no one is just gonna give us shit."

"Well, we have bikes. Maybe we could run an errand or something for them?"

Andy shook his head and peddled on. "Fuck it."

"Katie, grab my fanny pack." Chad diligently wiped gun oil down his AR-10.

"When are we going out dad? I'm getting stir crazy in here."

Steve walked into the garage. His heavy boots thudded against the wooden step from the lobby. "I agree. We're low on water and I need to get out for a stroll."

Chad looked up from cleaning his gun, "I work best with just Katie."

"Hey, don't worry about me. Besides, if I get killed, one less person eating our supplies."

Chad frowned and looked back to his weapon. "I'm not taking anyone but Katie."

"Fuck you, Ranger boy," Steve growled, storming out of the garage and back into the living area. "You're not the only person with survival skills."

"Then fucking go out by yourself and stop pestering me like a ten year old."

Katie scooted a red milk crate over and plopped down on it. She unfastened the straps on the pack and looked inside.

"Might be good to have another set of eyes."

"I'm not interested in an argument, Katelyn."

"So what, Dad? You're just mad that you're running low on hot sauce packets."

"What?" Chad snatched the fanny pack and quickly looked inside. "Fuuuuck."

Katie laughed.

"Doesn't matter. We need to keep moving. We have been at this old service station for a little over a week now."

"I'm sure Mom and Macy are fine. We don't live in town and that's where all the monsters come from."

Chad pinched his brow, "Katie. I love you. But, let's be real. Have you seen anyone under age thirteen since this shit went down?"

"No, but—"

"And how old is your sister?"

"She's ten, but—"

"And do you think your mother would shoot Macy if she turned, or try to help her?"

Katie didn't reply. She stared off into the dimly lit garage in silence. The quiet sunbeam that peeked through the boarded windows highlighted small particles of dust that danced about.

Chad stood and clipped his belt. "Squirrel, there is a chance they're fine. But, we need to be ready to face the reality that something has happened to them."

Katie just stared at the dancing dust.

"This is the research and development laboratory," Sammy smiled and gestured into the room. Several men and women in lab coats moved about a fairly clean make shift lab. They had several computers up and running, some microscopes, beakers, and other lab supplies.

"What are you researching?" Shane scratched his head.

"They do all kinds of stuff from weapons to the virus itself. It might not be much, but they have been a huge help in developing the Rattler Corp."

"The Rattle Corp?" Artez chuckled."What is that?"

Remember when you were first coming into the compound with the ferals hot on your ass?"

"Yes," Shane answered, annoyed.

"And do you recall that car with the dangling chains?"

"Yes." Artez smiled.

"They developed that."

"Chains?" Shane mumbled and shook his head.

"No, stupid. They captured a live feral and discovered that it can be distracted with loud noises. Ragers are much more resistant to such tactics."

"Yeah, stupid." Artez laughed.

"Well, we have a lot of other divisions, too." Sammy snapped, clearly annoyed.

"Alert, Alert, Alert." The intercom system blasted."Armed vehicles approaching the gate."

"Figures," Sammy mumbled bolting off down the hall."Probably people from crazy town."

"Crazy town?" Artez repeated.

One of the women in lab coats ushered them out of the lab."Yes, it's what we call the small town northwest of here. They have a crazy mayor that thinks God is punishing the earth and we're all blasphemers."

"Lovely."

"We've had small skirmishes with their zealots in the past. A few of them claim to wield the power of God."

"Great."

"The name is Sarah, by the way. Sarah Corso. If you find anything weird or interesting, make sure you bring it to me. Whether it be biological or mechanical. But, I prefer biological."

"Sarah, we need to lock down the lab."

"Good luck, boys."

The heavy iron doors of the lab closed and Shane could

hear locks being secured.

Dozens of people in red and black tactical uniforms rushed past the pair. Artez grabbed the arm of an old man in his late forties. He wasn't running like the others. He was calmly walking in the opposite direction. His graying beard and glasses were in stark contrast with most of the other members. He wore an odd vest that was covered in weird tools and gadgets.

"Can I help you two?"

"Yeah, what do we do while this Alert is going on."

"No clue."

Shane smiled."I'm former military and he is a police officer. We're useful."

"Not to me."

"Huh?"

"I'm AOE-128 robotics division. They call me Techit."

"Robots?"

"Yeah, Robots. So if you're not a robot, you're useless to me."

Shane and Artez glanced back and forth between once another.

"You want to see 'em?"

All three men smiled.

Sammy quickly climbed the metal stairs of the east oil tower. She kept one hand on the metal, rust-flaked rail and the other on the strap of her rifle. She reached the top and stepped from the grated stairs to the smooth top of the giant white storage tank. Moving to the center, she lowered her rifle just as three white vehicles pulled up outside of the chain link fence. She popped the covers on her scope and began checking ranges. The vehicles were well armored with thick quarter inch steel pates welded in several areas. The tires were protected and the drivers had to peer out of small narrow slits. The vehicles were all white with bright red crosses painted inside a yellow star on the doors and the hood. A man in dirty white robes and a short beard stepped from the car. He had some sort of gnarled looking staff that clumsily caught on the car door as he stepped out. *Classic,* Sammy thought to herself. *Fucking classic...*

"I'll head out to see him," Joseph held his arms out as several ZOD members strapped a ballistic vest to his body.

"Sir, I must advise against this. This group has been violent in the past," the woman protested.

Joseph ran his hands through his thinning hair."We got Sammy on the tower, right?"

"Yes, and three others. But, you are the leader of this chapter. We can't afford to lose you."

"Well, if I get attacked make sure she kills the guy with the stick."

"But, Sir—"

Joseph raised his hand and silenced her."This town is violent and we have had clashes in the past. Maybe this will be our chance to make peace with them."

Several men and women clad in red and black tactical gear moved around hurriedly. They held their weapons at ready and stepped out from the iron door with the ZOD. Joseph stepped out into the afternoon sun. He held his hand up to shade his eyes and walked toward the fence. Two armed men walked alongside of him, their weapons at ready.

"Greetings Mister Paradis," the man in white robes spoke softly.

"How did you know my name?" Joseph was taken aback.

"I know much of your band of heathens."

"Our group exists to offer protection from the monsters that have plagued our lands. We would even offer to help your city if—"

"We have no need of your help. We have God helping us."

Joseph ran his hand through his thinning hair."If you don't want our help, why are you here?"

A light wind picked up and blew the zealot's dirty white

robes around him."I'm here in the name of our Lord and Savior. Put down your weapons, come out of your den of wickedness and perversion, and offer yourselves to me."

Joseph chuckled,"You come here to our home in robes and a stick, insult us, our efforts, and now demand our surrender?"

"No, I come with the word of God Almighty. You have turned against his word and have become an abomination. Your group must repent or face righteous judgment."

"We're a freedom fighting group that is designed to help people find resources and freedom from oppression."

"You've been warned. If you continue to refuse the Lord God, he will bring a plague down upon you."

Joseph chuckled,"You mean like the end of civilization or virus infected monsters that attack and eat people? I'm pretty sure we have found the method of surviving that."

"Both! The Lord God demands your-"

"Get the fuck out of here. We don't need your superstitions, old man."

"You dare to bring judgment and death on your people? A death for which there will be no repentance?"

Joseph walked back to the chain link fence. He felt an eerie coolness wash over him. He had never been a religious man. But, this nut job scared him a little bit. "What? Do you think you're God?"

The old man opened the car door and stood with his foot on the inside step."No, I am not God. But, God has ordained me to be as a god. And for that, I will wield his judgment. Because of your hardened heart, I will bring His wrath down on you and your ZOD group."

"Do your worst, old man. Your magic doesn't scare me. You're not God." Joseph secured the gate and walked back to the compound.

"I will be a made God. I will be his wrath."

The thick metal doors were closing and Joseph smirked while raising his middle finger.

"Dude, this is freaking cool!" Artez kneeled and ran his calloused hand over the top of T3-ZD.

Rich smiled, moving the large radio controls in his hand. T3-ZD whirled and spun."Totally remote controlled."

Shane frowned,"So exactly how long does it live when a rager completely smashes it apart?"

Rich flipped a lever and small pistol popped out of a hatch on top."It has a means to defend itself. It's not going to take one out, but it has grenades in a rollout ramp in its base. It can survive a blast directly under it. Ragers—not so much."

Artez's eyes lit up,"Oh, hold up, homie. I know what it is. That's a T3 robot from Star Wars! Isn't it!?"

Rich smiled,"It is. I modified the structure with reinforced plating. It can survive a direct grenade hit nine out of ten times. It is all but bullet proof everywhere except its joints."

"Neat!"

"And most neat of all," Rich continued,"Is that I can build it with basic parts we scavenge. I can use a CPU from just about any basic shit computer. So, plenty of repair parts."

Shane was unimpressed."So, it's only way to cripple—not even kill—a rager is to blow itself up?"

"Well, it doesn't kill itself. I mean—"

"Can it even right itself if knocked over?"

Rich nodded,"It can. It has a fully flexible torso with independent armatures. The only real limitation is that it can only operate on smooth surfaces—like roads. But, in case you noticed, DARPA shut down when the world did. So how about you not bust my balls."

"I'm just saying."

Rich motioned to a large thick wooden table covered with parts, motors, and scrap metal."If you can build better, have it. It's not like I have the resources the Springfield MO guys have."

"What do you mean?"

Rich made gestures with his hands."They got these hydraulic suits. They call them ORBS—"

"ORBS?" Shane arched his eyebrow skeptically."How did they build those with industry and stuff down?"

THE APOCALYPSE OF ENOCH

"Before the fall, ZOD was made up of the top geeks and nerds in the nation. I first built T3-ZD before shit hit the fan. Anycase, ORBS is an acronym for Outbreak Response Battle Suit."

"Sounds intense."

"I've never seen them in action," Richard slowly smiled,"But, I have heard that a single ORBS unit has slaughtered hundreds of Ragers."

Artez nudged Shane in the ribs."How about that, Army boy?"

Shane rolled his eyes."Go find a donut."

Artez laughed and looked at Rich,"Shane can barely build a stiff drink."

"I'll have you know I was a trained bartender before the…" He trailed off. The light hearted mood suddenly took a serious turn. All three men thought about lives before, loved ones, lost, and how things would never be again.

"Well…" Rich paused."We all were somebody. What matters now is that we come together."

All three nodded with a half-hearted smile.

"For if God spared not the angels that sinned, but cast them down to hell, and delivered them into chains of darkness, to be reserved unto judgment."

2 Peter 2:4

2
RISE OF THE NEPHILIMS

"Yeah, I got fucking watch duty again tonight!" Sammy groaned into her radio, looking up at the starry night sky.

"The new guys from the ship are pretty cool. One of them is a cop and another is an army guy. Both are cleaning up down here at pool. Wish you were off. We could hustle them."

"I wish, Justin. I wish."

"Maybe tomorrow night?"

"Not then, either. Supreme Masterlord Paradis has us all on high alert because of them crazies."

"Don't be too hard on them. They haven't hurt anyone and at least they believe in something after this hell hole the world has become."

"They haven't killed anyone we know. You know how them religious crazies get. It won't be long and they will be stoning women and raping ten year olds they marry and all that."

"That's a little extreme—even for you."

"Well, ...I'm just saying."

"Shit!" Sammy ducked low. A soft red light shined down on her black t-shirt.

"What's wrong?" Justin asked from the other end of the radio.

The light shined down in front of her. She glanced out into the night and grabbed the radio. "I think someone had a laser site trained on me," she whispered. "Not sure."

"Fuck, call it in!"

Sammy looked down at the rusted and flaky white paint on the tanker tower. Wherever she looked, it lit up with a soft red glow.

"Call it in, Sammy. ...are you there?"

Shit, it's coming from me.

"Sammy I'm getting help."

"Wait." Sammy looked around to make sure it wasn't something else. But, everywhere her eyes fell, a soft red glow lit up. "Yeah, it's coming from me. I feel so stupid."

"Doooood. You had me freaked out."

"Yeah, me too. Weird thing is, I can't figure out what's glowing."

"Is it your watch?"

"No, it's coming from my head or something."

"Well, be careful."

Sammy ran her hands over her head. *I don't feel anything.* "Um, yeah. See ya' in the morning." *Where is that light coming from?*

"Taylor?" George called out quietly from below the tanker tower ladder.

Sammy looked over the edge. "Yeah?"

"I was sent out here to check on you. Justin Fank said you saw a light or something—wait, what's glowing on your face?"

Sammy slung her sniper rifle over her shoulder and started down the ladder. "Hell if I know. I'm coming down. I think maybe a lightening bug died in my hair or something."

"I can see it from here. That's one hell of a lightning bug."

Sammy hopped down the last two rungs and wiped the long blond hair from her face, "Okay, what is it."

George's eyes went wide and he covered his mouth.

"What?" Sammy's heart raced.

"Your eyes... They're glowing."

"What?" Sammy wiped her eyes with her hands and then looked at them. Her wet hands gave off a soft red glow. "Oh shit."

"Did you get your chem light in them or something?"

"No. I don't think so. I mean, those are for emergency use."

George gently hooked Sammy's arm, "Let's get you to sick bay and get your eyes flushed."

Sammy nodded, "I just don't remember messing with the glow stick."

They walked through the lower double doors. Sammy squinted her eyes. The lights were so bright. She lifted her hand up to her fore head to shield them.

"What's going on?" The guard closed the double doors behind them.

"Not sure, we need to get her to sick bay to get her eyes flushed."

Sammy felt a little chilled but slid out from under George's aid. "My damn legs ain't broke. And why is it so bright in here?"

"We need to hurry, I think the phenol is burning your eyes."

Sammy struggled to keep her eyes open. Murmured voices echoed in the distance and seemed to be far away. She started to feel dizzy. "I don't feel good."

"Bring her in here."

Sammy felt herself being laid back on a hard table. Maybe it was her bunk without the mattress? She tried to open her eyes, but the lights were blinding. "Turn the lights down—or out—or something."

"Sarah, something's wrong with her."

Sarah narrowed her eyes and looked down through her glasses. She lifted Sammy's lids and shined a small pen light in them. "Looks normal. Other than her pupils being dilated like someone on heroine."

George groaned and flipped the light switch. "Look at them now."

Sarah lifted Sammy's lid again and jumped back in surprise. Soft red light came out of her eyes. "Holy hell."

"What's wrong with me?" Sammy groaned and rubbed her eyes. "I feel drunk and cold."

"Look at that!" George pointed to Sammy's hands where she wiped her eyes. A small smear of glowing fluid coated the inside of her thumb.

Sarah frowned. She took a piece of cloth and swabbed the fluid and put it in a small petri dish. "I think she may be infected. Secure her down and quarantine this area. Who touched her?"

"Just me." George said, sheepishly half raising his hand.

"George, I'm going to need you to lie down on this other bed. I plan to draw some blood and do a test."

George swallowed hard, "Do you need to shackle me down?"

"I don't know, George. Do I need to shackle you down?"

"No Ma'am."

"Good."

"Sir, the medical division thinks Sammy is infected."

Joe looked up from his desk and rubbed his hands through his thinning blond hair. "Was she bit?"

"No. The report says no signs of topical infection."

"Not even a bug bite?"

"No, Sir."

"Well, that's easy. Just wait a few hours and then put her down if needed. Shame to lose her, though. She was one of our best shots."

"Um, Sir. That's what they wanted me to tell you. ...well, you might want to just take a look yourself."

Joe dropped his pen in frustration. "It's not that big of a deal. We lose a person or two a month. It sucks, but this is the world we live in. I don't need to see her."

"Sir, it's just..."

"Just what?" Joe was getting irritated.

"Just that medical thinks this is a new strain and wants your thoughts."

"Okay, tell Sarah I'll be right there." Joe finished tallying the numbers on fuel rations before putting the files into the drawer. He grabbed his hat and strode from his office, locking it behind him.

He started down the hall toward medical. There was a

significant crowd outside. "Make a hole."

The ZOD members moved aside quickly for their leader. "Is it true?"

Joe went to the door and entered in his combination on the keypad. "Is what true?"

"That Sam has been infected? She's our best shot."

Joe shrugged. "I'm about to find out. But, if she is—she 'was' our best shot." Joe went in and closed the door, silencing the complaints and groans and arguments on her behalf. To his surprise, the inside of the medical wing had been roped off with plastic. Several of his medical officers were wearing sealed suits and were tending to Sam and George.

Sarah's white lab coat was stained with over use. "Thanks for coming down."

"Well, it seemed important. Are we going to lose her?"

Sarah shifted her weight and down turned the corner of her mouth. "Maybe. Here is what I found. She is infected—but not with anything we have seen before."

"Just put her down. What about George?"

"He isn't infected, but we have him under observation for a few more hours. We think Sammy may have been incubating this virus for a while. We want to make sure George isn't a carrier before we let him from quarantine."

Joe frowned. "Maybe put them both down. Better safe than sorry."

Sarah gasped, "She is still aware and George is fine so far."

"So far."

Sarah's voice cracked. "Joe, I have known Sammy a long time. ...WE have known her a long time. And George heads up the chemical division. His guys make our chemlights and the ever popular mojo brew."

"I know who the fuck they are and what they do!" Joe snapped. "This is no different from when we had to put Mark, Julie, or Edwards down. This is no fucking different than losing Gerry or Ruby. Do your Goddammed job."

Sarah fought tears as Joe stormed from the room. Courtney stepped from the sealed bed and pulled the heavy plastic mask and helmet off. She vigorously ran her hands through her wavy brown hair. "What's up?"

"He said to put them down."

"Harsh." Courtney set the helmet on the table. "So, an injection of pentobarbital or sodium thiopental?"

"Just hold off. If anyone asks, I have it scheduled for in the morning but don't do anything until I get back."

"You got it." Courtney picked up a clipboard and examined the notes. "This virus chain must be new."

Sarah started to open the lab door, "You have no idea."

"Look at all of 'em." Zehner whispered looking through the boarded windows of the service station. "Katie and Chad are screwed."

Ashlee rubbed her hands together nervously. She gazed out across the tall grass field at several dozen hulking ragers jogging across the field. "I've never seen more than one or two together. Normally they fight."

"Wait," Steve narrowed his eyes and strained to see on the horizon. "I think I see a whole pack." He sprung up from the window and went to the ladder. "I bet there is going to be an epic battle. Let's go watch!"

Ashlee shook her head. "No way. I'm just going to relax here and wait for it to be over."

"Suit yourself." Zehner's heavy boots clanged against the metal ladder. He pushed the small aluminum hatch open and squinted under the dry hot Texas sun. Letting the hatch down slowly, he moved to the edge of the flat gas station roof. He could see the dozen or so ragers had crossed the field and were moving away. He brought his attention to the east at the other large group. They kicked up dust as they ran across the dry plains. *That's a good size group of ferals.* They extended on both sides of the road and were several hundred strong. Out in front of the group he saw two guys on the road. *Those guys are fucked.* He watched the pair as they neared. They apparently didn't see the ferals behind them. They just nonchalantly pedaled their bikes down the hot asphalt.

Zehner ran back to the aluminum hatch and yelled down. "Ashlee!"

"What?"

"We have two guys on bicycles heading this way. The ragers are gone, but the ferals are right behind them."

"We have everything barred down. I think we'll be able to hold them off." She more asked than told.

"Yeah, but I think we should try and help those guys."

"We don't know them, Steve."

"So?"

"So, helping them could get us killed. If not by the ferals getting in—they might be marauders."

"They'll be dead if we don't, so I'm helping." Zehner put the hatch back down and opened the crate on the roof. He pulled out the rifle and slapped the magazine into place. Moving to the side of the roof, he waved his hands back and forth to get the attention of the guys on the bikes.

"Another dust storm coming." Kurt sighed, peddling down the hot Texas road.

Andy glanced back. "I'm sick of these damn dust storms. At least this is a small one."

Kurt wiped sweat from his eyes, "That gas station is just a little bit away. Maybe we can find some water or something there—hide from the storm."

"Look, on the roof!"

Kurt skidded his bike sideways and propped it up with is prosthetic leg. "He has a gun. Be cool."

"I think he's waving or something?"

"What do you want to do?"

Andy glanced around—other than the rapidly approaching dust cloud, there wasn't much other than small dry brush and dirt. "Not much else around here."

Kurt squinted in the bright midday sun. "Looks like he's excited... Is he waving us in?"

"Looks like it."

"Well, just be cool. If the guy is weird as shit and we need to take him out, just follow my lead. If I say, Dad would have liked that—that means I'm going to hit him."

"Got it."

The pair pushed off and started pedaling toward the service station.

Those dumb fuckers don't know the ferals are behind them. Steven jumped and waved as excitedly as he could, yet the pair just continued to nonchalantly peddle toward the service station. He thought about firing a shot, but that would likely just bring the ferals down on them. It was then horror set in. If they didn't get here soon enough, the monsters would both catch them and kill them, or they would lead the ferals right into the station. *Oh fuck, oh fuck, oh fuck.*

"That guy is crazy, bro. Maybe we should just ride past."

Kurt nodded, "Something's up. Maybe he hasn't seen real people since the fall?"

"Maybe."

"Which means he has a fuckton of supplies stored up."

"Or he lures random passersby's and eats them." Andy chuckled. The thought that could actually be true caused his laugh to trail off.

"The fucked up part is that could easily be true."

"Yeah, I was just thinking that. So, do we just ride past?"

"I don't know, man. How long before we see another shelter? Have a chance for food— water?"

"Oh shit. Go! Fucking go, go go, GO!"

Kurt frowned as his brother started pedaling as fast as he

could. Kurt stood up on his bike, his prosthetic leg squeaked as pumped his legs to keep up, "What is it?"

"That's no dust storm! It's a pack of them beasts!"

Kurt looked back. Horror and fear ripped through him. He could see several hundred of the gray skinned infected people jogging towards them. They seemed tired and weak and were kicking up dust as their feet shuffled while they ran. Thick tan dirt covered their skin and torn ragged clothing. Their odd snarls and growls started to barely reach his ears. He peddled harder. The service station was nearing. "Just keep riding. Don't stop."

"What!?"

"That is a death trap."

"I'm stopping!" Andy shouted defiantly.

"If you do, you'll die."

Andy started to ride off of the road toward the station, but Kurt pedaled faster and kept going.

A single gunshot echoed out across the pains. Kurt skidded his bike to a stop. His brother climbed the hot guttering of the main building. *Dammit*. Kurt turned around and pedaled back. He jumped off of his bike and tossed it down. He stepped up on a power box and started to climb the guttering. "You just fucking killed us, Andy!"

Another shot tore out across the plains.

Zehner reached down and helped Andy to the flat roof. "There are guns in the crate there. Arm yourself."

Kurt took Zehner's hand and climbed up. Andy handed him a rifle. "Seem like a bad idea now?"

Kurt moved to the edge of the roof and stared out at the wave of ferals. He thought there were a hundred or so—but to his horror—the group was easily three times that. "No, now it seems like a terrible fucking idea."

"Load her up." Sarah nervously ran her fingers down her worn lab coat. Her voice was nervous and cracked in Chris

McQuillen's office. "She's sedated."

Chris frowned, "Why is Sammy in there tied up? ...and sedated?"

"We need to get to the Springfield, MO division. They have a full blown medical team and lab there."

Chris rested his hand on his batsaw. The saw blade bolted into the baseball bat had served him well in several battles with ferals. "So she is infected?"

Sarah glanced around in the pale light of the vehicle garage. "Yes, but not like we think. Her body fluids seem to give off some sort of bio-luminescence."

"So..." Chris stammered. "Is she still, ya' know. Still Sammy?"

"As far as I can tell."

"How long as she been infected?"

"At least 24 hours—but Astroth Paradis has ordered her terminated—George too."

"Wait, Canfield is infected?"

"No, that's the thing. He said to kill George because he was possibly infected."

"Wait, that would only happen if there was a quarantine."

Sarah shuffled nervously.

"You broke quarantine? Are you crazy?"

"No! That's what I'm saying. He ignored all the facts. Didn't even give me time to find out more, observe her, or anything."

"Sarah, this is insane. Even for you."

"Chris, what was I supposed to do?"

He took a deep breath and thumbed the edge of the saw blade. "Chris, this is Sammy and George we're talking about."

"So, how do you keep us from getting arrested, or worse, banished?"

Sarah handed him a clip board with a transfer order.

"You forged a transfer order?"

"I'm not sitting by while someone who just a few months ago dressed up and walked around with toy guns, decide if two of my friends die or not."

"Okay, I'm going to deny I knew anything."

"Fair enough."

Chris snatched the clipboard from Sarah and checked a

few more boxes. He walked out into the garage. Sammy was strapped down on a stretcher and George was sitting in a wheel chair, awkwardly protesting how he had two good feet to walk on.

"We have orders to transport Sammy and George up to the Springfield, MO medical division." Chris tossed the clipboard on his hood. "It's a long trip, so I want Scout-1 and Scout-2, Viper-1..."

"Viper one is still broke down. The welds on the axel aren't holding."

"Okay, then grab the Warthog."

"I'll anchor all the ZRV's and bring them," Levi hopped up from the counter.

Sarah smiled helped load Sammy from the stretcher to the back of Scout-1. She was bound by leather restraints and semi-conscious. Chris looked at her awkwardly. "She doesn't look any different."

Sarah climbed in the back seat and closed the door. "I have never seen her virus before. And had I not seen the bioluminescence first hand, I would not have believed it. It was like something out of a movie."

Chris started Scout-1 and his passenger side door opened. Artez climbed inside. He was fully dressed in ZOD tactical gear. "Nice to see you in your new digs, Artez."

"Yeah, just got them. We got wind of the trip. Shane, Tibbs, and Terry decided to come along. "

"Where are they?"

"Scout-2 and the Warthog."

The garage door opened and the small convey drove out into the hot Texas sun. The dark black tires crunched the hard clay earth. Chris slid a CD into the player. The stereo came to life. Chris smiled and bounced his fingers off of his steering wheel while Sarah nervously glanced back at the compound.

She expected alarm bells and sirens at any moment. Instead, she watched the tall petroleum towers faded into the horizon as the convoy sped north. They had made it. She dabbed Sammy's forehead with a damp towel. "Just hold on a while longer."

The ferals surrounded the building pretty quickly. They yanked and pulled on the wooden boards covering the windows. Bullets rained down from above, but seldom hit their mark. Instead, they ripped through fetid flesh that healed in seconds.

"I told you this was a bad idea!" Kurt took aim, pressing his sweaty cheek against his shoulder before depressing the trigger. The round tore through the jaw of a feral. The monster shrieked in pain and fell down amid the masses, only to be replaced by several others.

"This is pointless." Zehner groaned. "I'm going below and getting point blank." He lifted the aluminum hatch and started down the ladder.

Andy shrugged, "Might as well help."

Kurt exhaled deeply and followed them down into the service station. It was small. The ladder led down to a garage with all kinds of equipment and parts. He noticed several car batteries wired up to some sort of coil thing that was crammed into a huge blue plastic barrels of water. He tried to take a mental note of everything that was going on, but the growls of the ferals reaching through the windows, clawing and gnashing, were distracting him.

"Just point your rifle through the boards." Zehner demonstrated. The feral gnawed and bit at the barrel before its head exploded into a mass of flesh and gore. "Yup, I figured that would work much better."

"So how many do you have here?" Andy cast a nervous eye at the boarded windows wondering if they would hold.

"We have four. But, Chad and Katie are out and about. It's just me an Ashlee here now."

"She the one on the ground floor?" Kurt wiped sweat on his torn and ragged t-shirt.

"Yup." Zehner started toward the door to the lobby. "Ashlee, come meet our new friends."

Ashlee bursts through the door and slammed it shut. Her

long sweaty blonde hair hung between her breasts. Her shirt was ill fitting, hanging down in the front. "They're pulling on the boards!"

"What?" Zehner frowned and pushed passed her. He forced open the door and stood in disbelief. The ferals had pulled the boards off of the large display window and were trying to force their way through. He raised the rifle to his shoulder and fired a shot into the monster's head. The beasts fell dead, its hot red blood poured from the wound like watery syrup from a cup. "Quick! Get as many supplies as you can out of here and into the garage!"

Ashlee didn't move. She sat down on a dirty red tool box and stared into the distance.

Andy looked at Kurt and shrugged. They ran into the lobby and started grabbing boxes of foodstuffs. Zehner fired another shot into the head of a feral that had managed to squeeze through a torn board near the side window.

"We have had packs come through before, but they have never been smart enough to pull boards loose before." Zehner fired another round.

Ashlee screamed and shots echoed from the garage.

"Fuck." Zehner rushed to the door. "Keep shooting them as they come in." He jerked open the door. Ashley had her weapon up to her shoulder and was firing at a feral that had torn through and was rushing across the garage. He lifted his weapon up and fired. The rounds tore through the monster's body. It stumbled and growled, falling to the floor and knocking over a small metal toolbox. Another feral had already managed to get halfway through the door. Zehner grabbed her by the shirt and pulled her back through the door, slamming it shut.

Andy and Kurt were firing rounds through the boards, killing feral after feral.

"The fucking garage is lost." Zehner said with wide eyes. His voice became quiet amid the gun blasts. "We are lost."

"Fuck that." Kurt growled. He fired another shot. "We can hold this lobby. There are only three windows to defend."

Ashlee looked at Kurt with sad defeated eyes. "The ammo was in the garage. What we have is what we have."

"Fuck!" Andy ran his hands through his hair before lifting his rifle and shooting another feral. "What about hammers or something? We can try to barricade these windows again."

Kurt grabbed a small soda cooler and hoisted it up and slammed it against the third window on the west side. Zehner continued to fire shots while Ahslee tore through cabinets looking for nails and other tools. The growls and hammering of fists against the garage door seemed to sap the hope from everyone in the lobby.

"Not this way." Ashlee sobbed. "I don't want it to end this way."

"Pull it together, Ash." Zehner yelled, holding the cooler up against the window against the pushing and gnashing of the feral horde. "We're not lost yet!"

Ashlee shook her head softly. She leaned against the counter and placed her rifle in her mouth.

Andy rushed toward her, but she squeezed the trigger. In a single gunshot, she was gone. Her lifeless form slipped to the floor, revealing blood and gore on the wall behind her.

"Goddammit, Ash!" Zehner screamed.

"Worry about her later." Kurt snapped, smashing a claw hammer into the head of a feral that had pried a second board loose from the window.

"I'm out!" Andy smashed the butt of his empty rifle into the face and hands of a feral pulling on the north window boards."

"How many more are there?"

"Too many." Zehner shook his head. "Too goddammed many."

"Hold it together." Kurt fired another shot into the face of a feral.

The ferals growled and the boards of the large front window snapped. Several ferals fell through and onto the floor, cutting Steve off from Andy and Kurt. Kurt and Andy backed behind the counter toward the small office. Andy swung his empty gun like a club, bashing the head of the nearest feral and backing into the doorless office. Zehner screamed and fought for a few more seconds before going silent and sliding down under the mass of hungry fingers and gnashing teeth.

"You mother fuckers!" Kurt fired another round into the

face of a feral while Andy screamed and swung his gun like a mad man. One snagged his pant leg and Andy stumbled back into Kurt. He slipped to one knee and ignored the stinging hot pain as the beast bit into the flesh of his leg. He kicked and punched, slamming the butt of the gun into the monster's head. It fell unconscious only to be replaced by two more. Kurt fired another shot.

And as suddenly as they rushed into the room, the ferals all stopped in unison. Andy pushed one back out of the office, ignoring the dozen or so bites on his arms and legs. He brought the butt of the blood smeared into the head of the beast that just stood there. It offered no resistance and fell to the floor. Kurt raised his rifle and fired a shot into another one. The monster didn't flinch. It simply went limp and fell. There were maybe a dozen of the beasts in the gas station lobby and all of them stared off into the distance as in a daze. They didn't growl or snarl. The only indication they were alive were the rapid rise and fall of their chests. "What the fuck is wrong with them?" Andy grimaced, shaking the blood from his arms.

"Who cares. Take 'em out!"

They attacked the monsters relentlessly and quickly, dropping every one of them in the lobby. To their surprise the ones outside standing motionless as well. "Check the garage."

Andy cautiously opened the door. There were probably forty ferals in the garage, all staring off into the distance.

"Clear them out, too?"

"Fuck that. Get to the roof!"

The pair erupted from the thin aluminum hatch and collapsed on the hard flat brown pebbled surface after securing the hatch. "Holy fuck that was a close one."

Andy gingerly removed his shirt. "Damn, those things can bite."

Kurt laid on his back and marveled that they had survived. Andy was weak but had a wry smile on his face. Kurt chuckled, "Remember that hot model you dated? What was her name?"

"Which one? You know I'm the better looking brother."

Kurt propped himself upon his elbows, "The biter. She left bigger marks than those things."

"Ha! You mean, Kelley? I miss her. She was awesome."

Kurt crawled to the edge of the service station and peered over. "Damn, there are a lot of them."

Andy struggled to the edge, tearing his shirt into strips. "Wow. I don't think I have ever seen so many. Maybe three hundred?"

"About that."

"We barely put a dent in them. Why do you think they just stopped?"

"No clue. And all at the same time? That's fucking weird."

"Well, I'm not moving from this roof until they're all gone."

"Ha!" Andy pointed. "Look."

The ferals suddenly came to life and ran away to the west as fast as they ran to the station.

"Now THAT is weird." Kurt smiled weakly.

THE APOCALYPSE OF ENOCH

"And the Lord said, I will destroy man whom I have created from the face of the earth; both man, and beast, and the creeping thing, and the fowls of the air; for it repenteth me that I have made them."

Genesis 6:7

3
COME TO ME

"Dad, is that a factory?"

Chad lifted his rifle scope and peered into the distance. Brown stone and a smoke stack, stained with black around the top, poked out over the trees. "Katie, I think it is."

"Do we want to head to it, or head back?"

"We're closer to it than the station. Let's go check it out. I'd hate to get caught on the road at night."

Katie smiled, slinging her rifle over her back. Her shotgun stuck out from her back case far above her head, like a thick black flagpole with no flag. "I don't know, Dad. I don't think we're going to find any taco sauce packets there."

"Well, I don't think they will have any nail polish either, cupcake."

"How do you know? It could be a nail polish factory."

"Not likely," Chad said with a chuckle. "But I if we're dreaming, I'm wishing for a car manufacturing plant."

They made their way through the sparse forest. The trees were thin and wispy. The land had more tall bushes than trees and the dry ground created small dust clouds with every step. Katie snacked on red mulberries. She liked traveling with her dad. She knew that the land was dangerous now, but she could always let her guard down a little bit when they traveled. The pair paused about a quarter of a mile from the factory.

"Looks old, Dad."

"Yeah, surely not a car or nail polish factory."

Katie popped her scope covers and lifted her rifle to her shoulder. She scanned the top of the three story brick structure. "Looks real old, Dad."

Chad peered through his scope at the windows, "Not a shred of glass in the windows unless it is that reinforced chicken wire type stuff.. This is a real old structure. It's been abandoned a long time."

Katie moved her scope down and around the floors. "I see graffiti."

"Old or new?"

"How do you tell?"

Chad spied a small pile of black rock that sat at the base of an old rusted out auger. "Look for chips in the paint, brightness, water marks, or moss. That sort of thing. Context if possible."

"Looks old then."

"I think this is an old coal mine." Chad looked at the ground to see if he could see any foot prints or vehicle tracks.

"I don't see anyone around."

"Yeah, looks deserted. I don't see any footprints of vehicle marks around the outside."

Katie lowered her scope. She pulled out her magazine and started counting ammo. "Ammo check."

Chad smiled. His daughter might only be fourteen, but she was adjusting to this world well. "I have sixty two AR rounds, forty five forties."

Katie placed her magazine back in her rifle, "I have thirty AR, thirty forty cal, and twenty five twelves."

"Looks like we're good. I'll take point coming in. Let's go south wall."

"Okay."

They made their way around the old mine. Some of the large windows were completely collapsed. The old tan bricks had crumbled and fallen, leaving small piles in the dirt around it. Small bits of coal and other material were mixed in with the surrounding hard dry Texas dirt. The building was three stories and there was a separate large cylinder smoke stack that extended about sixty feet above the top floor. It was in remarkably good condition. They sat and watched the building for about thirty minutes.

Confident there was no one inside, Chad emerged from the weeds and rushed to the south wall. He quickly poked his head inside one of the large empty windows. It looked like the inside of the structure had burned at some point and then was completely cleared out. No wiring, so flooring, no plaster or dry wall. Just brick walls and concrete floors. He motioned and Katie came rushing from the tree line to his side.

"Pretty cleared out. Let's make our way to the third floor and find a good place to hunker down for the night."

"Any signs of squatters?"

Chad shook his head and stepped through the large window. His AR was lifted to his shoulder and in the ready. Katie slid her AR under her arm and tightened the strap before pulling her shotgun. Her Benelli would serve her the best in the tight quarters.

The room opened up into a small hall. Holes in the concrete walls and above the doors revealed that even the pipes had been removed. "This place has been cleaned out good."

"What do you mean, Dad?"

Chad motioned to the holes above the door near the ceiling. "Pipes and such went through there. This is a super old building. I think it doubled as a mine and a power plant. Maybe just a power plant."

"So, there were wires in there?"

"No, most likely hot water pipes for the radiators."

"Like in a car?"

"No, like in grandma's house. They generated hot water and steam and that was collected in the large metal coils that heated the rooms."

Chad moved into the breezeway. Metal framed stairs with concrete steps rose to his left. To his right was the breezeway to large double door entry. The doors had long since been removed. Dirt and a few small plants littered the floor.

Katie put her shotgun back in its holster and brought up her rifle. She lifted it to her shoulder and kneeled, scanning the treeline. "Clear."

Chad hustled up the first flight of stairs. He turned and trained his weapon just over the top of the second portion.

THE APOCALYPSE OF ENOCH

Katie transitioned back to her shotgun and ran up behind him. He moved up the stairs slowly and she followed, but backwards. Keeping her shotgun at ready and covering their rear.

The second floor was much like the first except the rooms were larger. They made their way to the third floor. The rooms were much larger and expansive, four in all. But the ceiling was missing and much of the floors were covered in bricks and debris. "I would have thought the larger rooms would have been on the bottom."

Katie shrugged. "Is that bad? I mean, more dangerous?"

"Not really."

"But, if it rains we'll be wet as a drowned whistle."

"Dad, I think it has only rained once this week. I bet we're safe."

Chad grinned and shook out his bed roll. The setting sun had just dipped below the horizon. "Just means we're due."

"So, we're camping here?"

"Well, at the edge of this room we can see the stairs." He pointed to a small rusted metal rebar sticking out of the west concrete wall. "That's a good way to climb to the top if we want to scout to the west in the morning."

Katie looked up at the dimming sky. The bright blue was fading into dark and the first twinkling of stars were starting their silent song. "I miss home, Dad."

Chad gave her a hug. He felt her clinging to him for security, for protection, for companionship. His little girl was growing up in a horrible world. She would never have a prom. She would not have a first date. She likely would not make it to her thirtieth birthday if she wasn't careful. Chad knew they couldn't make it on their own. They needed a community. Some security.

"Dad?" Katie said, not breaking the long overdue hug.

"What?"

"You kind of stink."

Chad laughed. "Well, you're not some fresh thing either, missy."

Katie laughed and unpacked her ruck. She pulled out a can of corn and scratched it back and forth over the concrete floor, slowly peeling the thin aluminum edges away. She gave it a light squeeze and popped the top. "Dad. We need a bow."

"A bow?"

"Yeah, so we can hunt and not stress over using up our ammo."

Chad laid on top of his sleeping bag and pulled his hat over his eyes. "You take first watch. Wake me about 2 am or when you get real tired."

Katie checked her watch. It was eight thirty. She contemplated what life would be like in ten years when batteries and the last remnants of her childhood faded away. "Dad?"

"Yes?" Chad answered from under his hat.

"I was thinking."

"And?"

"In five years, maybe ten—all of the batteries and stuff from my life will be gone. I'll be an adult."

"Yes, probably."

"So, is this what it's like when you got old and the pay phone vanished?"

Chad laughed. "Shut up, Katie."

"I'm just trying to see what it's like to be old."

"Quit while you're ahead."

Katie laughed and finished her can of corn.

Artez fumbled with the paper map he found in the glove box of Scout-1. "So, we should be coming up on Harlington?"

"Harlingen. It's a small city. We haven't had a single refugee from there, so I can't imagine anything good being there. We're going to take the bypass around the city." Chris bobbed his fingers to the music.

"Probably for the best. I don't like the idea of an interstate though. Saint Louis was bumper to bumper."

"Oh, it's not that big. It's a bypass, but just a divided road. No rails or anything. Harlingen isn't that big."

"Doesn't take many cars to clog up a road. ...I'm just saying."

"She is coming to," Sarah dabbed Sammy' forehead.

"Sammy?"

Sammy weakly opened her eyes. "Where am I?"

"Sammy, this is Sarah. We're on our way to the medical division in Springfield, MO."

Sammy sat up. She tried to wipe her sweaty hair from her eyes but the leather restraints kept her hands at her hips. "What? Why am I tied up?"

"You're infected, Sammy."

"How?"

"We're not sure. But your body fluids have bioluminescence."

"I KNEW I hadn't been careless with my chemlight."

Sarah frowned. "Sammy, did you hear what I said — you're infected."

"Well, if I was going to turn into a feral or rager, I would have done that by now."

"And if you were a giggler, it takes about two weeks." Artez quipped.

"A giggler?" Chris asked skeptically. "What the hell is a giggler?"

"Man, I don't know. We had a guy on our boat from some sort of comedy troupe get infected. Took him like two weeks to change and it made him laugh — a lot. It was creepy as fuck. It must of hit his nervous system somehow."

"Did we know this?" Chris looked at Sarah in the rearview mirror.

"Kind of. I didn't know it was a different kind of feral. I thought that was just something new."

"So, these gigglers are what killed Ruby, Gerry, and the others?"

"Maybe?" Sarah's voice waivered. "We didn't get any of them to sample.

Sammy itched her face with her shoulder. "So, how do you know I'm infected?"

Because she can sense your superiority.

"I saw the virus in your blood, Sammy."

Sammy frowned. "I'm not superior to anyone. And is there a cure?"

Sarah sighed, "Not yet. But, you are not turning into a monster so you may be a link to finding a cure."

Sammy yawned, "I'm really tired."

"It may be the virus sending your system out of whack. Are you hungry?"

"No." Sammy said, laying on her back. She relaxed and closed her eyes. She crossed her feet and placed them in Sarah's lap. "I'm just going to take a nap. Wake me up if something exciting happens."

Rest. Soon your transformation will be complete.

"Whatever." Sammy groaned. "Just don't shoot me while I sleep."

"What is she talking about?" Artez glanced nervously over his shoulder.

"Or who is she talking to?" Chris griped his steering wheel. "And how do we know she isn't contagious?"

Sarah cleared her throat, "Because the virus was binding to her chromosomes and not individual cells."

"Wait, that doesn't make sense." Artez argued. "Viruses are not even the same size, let alone work like that."

"I don't have time to give you a medical degree," Sarah argued, "But, for the most part you are correct. But this one is working differently. It's in her cells, but it is modifying her chromosomes and it is only attaching itself to the double X. I think men are going to be immune."

"That doesn't make a lick of sense, Sarah."

"Well, that's the best I can explain what I saw—which is why it is very important to get Sammy to the medical division as soon as possible."

"I think I should've stayed at the compound." Artez laughed.

Chris slowed at a four-way intersection. The lights were long since out and the roads were covered with debris and an occasional car. "Looks like last month's storm did a number on some of the houses here."

"Kinda' does. Makes me wonder how many years will go by before nature erases humans all the way?"

Chris turned north on the bypass, "I saw a pic from World War II where these cars were abandoned on a free way. It was some sort of traffic jam or something. Anycase, in about 80 years the road was a hundred percent covered in plants and some small trees had grown up through the cars."

"Well, I guess it's safe to say we won't be alive when nature has erased us."

"Guys, we don't know that humanity is over."

"She's right," Chris agreed. "The black plague killed like ninety percent of the world's people."

"No, not quite." Sarah countered. "It killed about eighty to ninety percent of Europeans. But, it only reduced the world population from about five hundred million to about three hundred fifty million, give or take."

"Either fucking way," Artez groaned, "It killed almost everyone in Europe."

"Yeah, but Europe still came back." Chris chuckled. "So, it's safe to say that we will come back."

"Yeah, well I didn't see any black death victims running around spreading this disease. They all just died. We have ferals, ragers, gigglers, and who knows what else."

Chris bit his lip and nodded, "A fair point."

"Guys." Sarah said incredulously, "Before we write off humanity, can we focus on the task at hand?"

"We're just talking." Artez said defensively.

"But, on another note—he could be right. Can anyone even have kids without them turning into little monsters?"

Sarah bit her lip, "I'm not sure. But, I bet the medical division has answers on that."

"Either way, this is going to be a long trip." Chris leaned back in his chair. "About that navigational plan?"

Artez flipped open the map and struggled to keep it unfolded. He spread it out on the dash and on his lap, "Okay, OKAY. I'm on it. Looks like we need to take either Interstate 77 or the frontage road to the north."

"Hmmm," Chris mumbled to himself, "I guess we will play it by ear."

Kurt opened his eyes. The dawn was breaking over the

eastern sky. The orange glow of the sun was washing away the dark blue of the night. He ignored the rumbling in his belly and sat up. He scooted to the edge of the building and glanced out over the plains. Not even a single sign of the hundred plus ferals that attacked him and Andy. ...ANDY.

Kurt looked back. His brother's torn shirt was on the roof, but Andy was gone. "Andy!" Kurt rushed to the hatch. It was unlocked. He lifted it and yelled down inside the garage, "Andy!"

Kurt climbed down the rusted metal ladder into the garage. "An—" his words trailed off and fell into a massive pit that opened up in his stomach. Andy hung from the cherry picker by a rope. His neck was bent and distended. His eyes were wide and bulging and his tongue was swollen and hanging from his mouth.

"No!" Kurt screamed and ran to his brother. He grabbed a cardboard knife off of the bench and jumped on it. He grabbed Andy by the arm and cut the rope. It snapped as it broke and the weight of Andy's body pulled Kurt from the bench to the garage floor. He hit the ground hard and shuffled to the top of his brother. He started to do chest compressions when he felt his body was cold and rigamortus was setting in. Kurt lifted his hands and scooted away from the body. He placed his face in his hands and cried. Kurt sat in the dark garage until the sun was well up into the morning sky. He gathered his wits and stood. His brother was gone. He was alone. He was going to have to gather supplies and keep going.

Kurt wiped tears from his eyes. The Texas sun was beating down on the tiny garage and he heat was starting to kick up. Kurt grabbed some ammunition, a rifle, and two pistols. He found a ruck sack and some other militaristic supplies. Rummaging through the tool bench, he found a note written on a vehicle service ledger.

"Dearest brother. Seems those bites were infectious. I told you they were zombies. ...guess I can't collect that bet. Besides, you are already riding the girl's bike. Short of making you carve a pirate leg, not much else I can do to make you pay. LOL. That being said, I'm changing. The

> bites have already healed, I have a monster fever and I'm hungry like a mofo.
> I guess you were right about you out living me. Prick.
> ...I don't know what the fuck to write. I miss dad. I miss mom. I'll miss you, but I won't miss the fucking world. I thought about shooting myself, but you were sleeping next to the ammo crate and I didn't want you to argue with me. I know you wouldn't let me kill myself and I don't think jumping off the roof would do much more than break my legs. (You know my luck). I figure this is the easiest way to go. As a joke, I was going to pull my pants down and spank it to go out Caradine style. But, I guess finding me wouldn't be very much fun for you. I'm sorry I have to do this. I just couldn't risk turning into one of those things and making you have to experience a bad movie cliché scene of shooting me or not shooting me.
> Just do me two things. One, always remember I love you. And two,
> STAY ALIVE.
>
> Love always,
> Andy

Kurt neatly and carefully took the note from the receipt book and folded it. He placed it into his shirt pocket and continued rummaging through the toolboxes. He found an old shovel and went outside. The hard dry Texas earth resisted his every attempt to dig into it. He stopped often—sometimes to cry--sometimes to stretch his aching back. The sun streaked across the sky. The small shovel slowly chipped away the dirt and pile grew and grew. Kurt took off his sweat soaked shirt and soaked it in the rain water catcher. He tied it around his head to keep him cool. He ignored the blisters that had grown so large they were bleeding. He kept digging. Andy deserved it.

At last the hot baking sun relented and started its descent into the western sky. Kurt finished digging and went back inside. He kissed his fingers and touched Andy's forehead. Sliding his body into a long blue plastic tarp, he drug it outside and gently place Andy into the grave. Kurt retrieved the receipt book and a pen. He sat down on the edge of the grave and wrote:

> Dearest Andy,
>   I just spent all day digging in the hot sun to bury your ass. I'm still pissed off you hung yourself, but thanks for saving me from the cliché movie decision. I see now you won the bet, but I still don't think they're zombies. But, to be fair, I'm going to call it a half win. To show my dedication, I'm going to keep riding that fucking girl's bike.
>   I don't know what else to say. It's getting dark, I'm tired, and I love you. I can't promise how long I'm going to stay alive in this world, but since it was your last request, I guess I have to give it my best go.
>
>   I miss you, brother.
>   ~Kurt

Kurt slid the note into a small plastic bag and stuck it in Andy's pocket. He gave him a final glance in the waning daylight before shoveling dirt back into his grave. The first shovel was the hardest. The finality of covering the grave with dirt set in. Kurt wanted to stop and rip Andy from the grave. He hoped that Andy would weakly whisper his name, that he was okay. That he was not dead. ...but he was.

Kurt finished covering the grave. He snapped the end of shovel off and emptied one of his canteens into the hard ground, softening it. He took the shovel handle and stuck it the ground, before using duct tape to affix a backwards license plate to the handle. With a black sharpie, he wrote "Andy Yaeger."

Kurt packed up the rest of his supplies and refilled his canteens in the rain water barrel. With a final look, he picked up the girls bike and started pedaling to the west. Nighttime or not, there was no way he was staying there and there was no way he was going to sleep.

THE APOCALYPSE OF ENOCH

"Ugh. I'm a hot mess." April disgustingly ran her fingers through her oily dirty hair.

Vorto looked up at her with his large dark eyes. He turned his head to the side in attempt to try and understand what she was saying.

"You are one creepy little thing. Do you know that?" April said with contempt. "Of all the traveling partners I get, it's a half kid monster tied to a lawn mower." She kept walking on the hot road, ducking in and around the occasional abandoned car.

Your general is coming.

"Huh?" April turned and looked at Vorto. "You can speak?"

Vorto glanced back up her and kept scooting himself across the cracked asphalt.

"Say it again." April narrowed her eyes.

Vorto squealed softly and lunged to the right, knocking himself over. His thin gray fingers snatched a grasshopper. He eagerly shoved it in his mouth and crunched down.

"Oh my God, Vorto. You straight up nasty. "

Vorto forced himself back upright and smiled at April. Dark black grasshopper juice and shell littered amid his teeth.

"Look, I heard your gross little bug eating behind say something about a general. Say it again."

Vorto smiled and started chewing the grass hopper again. "Oorooroo."

April shook her head and started walking. "This is hopeless."

Vorto scooted along behind her, keeping his dark eyes on the side of the road for more delicious bugs.

"Who the hell made you, anyway? I mean—look at you. You sure aint smart enough to make yourself."

I made him, just as I made you.

"What?" April whipped around. "Okay, now I know that wasn't you, Vorto." She couldn't see anyone behind her. "Okay, you. I'm armed. Wherever you are, come out or I put one in your ass." April pulled her pistol from under her shirt.

I am everywhere and I am nowhere. But for now, move from the road. Enemies approach and you are not yet strong enough to face them.

April ducked low and waved her gun around. Vorto covered his eyes and squealed at the sight of it. "I'm not playing!" She moved to the side of the road and crouched low looking for cover. "I'll shoot the hell out of your ass!"

Vorto scooted off the road and hid behind a bush. He growled and shook his finger into the air in support of April. "Rrrooorarwh!"

April moved off of the road, "Keep your eyes peeled, Vorto. We're being stalked."

Vorto nodded and smiled before being distracted by another bug. He scooted off across the hard dry dirt.

"Don't go too far, Vorto." April cautiously ducked low and followed.

April could hear the feint sound of vehicles. Her heart raced. She was both excited and fearful. She wasn't sure what was going on with her sickness. She didn't change like she expected to, but her saliva and eyes glowed like a glow stick. She was pretty sure she had a fever too, but she had been avoiding strangers. She looked down at Vorto and realized no one would do anything except try to kill him. She just couldn't take that chance. She decided to duck low and wait for the car to go by.

"Calling on Jesus." April muttered under her breath as a small convoy of vehicles drove by. They were all black and had the same logo on them as the car that was dragging the chains behind it when they left the ship near that industry shipyard on the river.

"Orroooya?" Vorto held a captured grasshopper up to April.

"Oh, gross!" She slapped Vorto's hand away. April turned back and watched the vehicles drive by. "ZOD? I remember them. Stephanie and Sinjin was in that group. She sure didn't like people like you, Vorto. Good thing we ducked off the side of the road."

April tucked her pistol back in her belt under shirt. "Come on, Vorto. Let's get moving."

"Arroooyouah" Vorto smiled and crunched on another grasshopper. He scooted across the ground with his knuckles.

"Wake up, Katie bug." Chad whispered.

Katie opened her tired eyes. Her father was kneeling over her with his index finger on her lips. "What do we have?"

"Not sure. I'm guessing one of them feral people," he whispered.

Katie could hear something rustling through debris on the bottom floor. "Coons?"

Chad shook his head. "I don't think so. I want you to go to the south wall, tie off on the rebar, and set up. If shit hits the fan, repel off of the wall and reassess."

Katie got up quickly and gathered up her supplies. Chad slipped on his ruck and moved to the doorway and peered down the stairs. He tilted his ears toward them and tried to listen to how many he thought there might be. He shook his head and slowly and quietly moved over to Katie's position. "Sounds like a hell of a lot more than one. I didn't hear any voices, which means it's some of the infected."

"Great." Katie rolled her eyes. "Do you think they'll come up here?"

"Let's hope not. But, if they do—" Chad pointed to a crumbled pile of debris. "See that brick pile?"

"Yes."

"That is your threshold. If a single one of them gets past that pile, repel over the side."

"What are you going to do?"

Chad hooked his rope around a twisted bit of rebar and used a D clip to clock it down. "I'll be right behind you."

For several minutes the soft shuffles of feet and occasional sound of debris being scurried about echoed from below. Katie groaned under breath. "I just wish they would either go away, or come up here. The wait is killing me."

Chad smiled through the tension. Every encounter with the infected people was a dangerous one. Yet, he was confident in their shooting skills to see them through. What concerned him the most was the number he expected to be rummaging below. It would be challenging for even them to handle. "Be patient, Katie. Likely they will get bored and move along."

Katie looked east. The night sky was starting to lighten and the tale tell glow of the eastern sun was beginning to light up the horizon. She scratched at a small clod of dirt that had stuck itself to the stock of her rifle. "Well, at least my harness is comfortable."

Chad pointed to the doorway of the crumbled room. He lifted his rifle up to his shoulder. Katie propped herself up on the edge of the roof with her hard soled boots and leaned back over the edge. She ignored the anxiety of her rope being the only thing that kept her from falling to her death.

"I'll shoot first. "

Katie felt her palms get sweaty. She took one hand off of her rifle and wiped it on her pants. She switched hands and repeated. She lifted to rifle to her shoulder when the monster broke the door frame. It was massive. She had seen them before, but this one seemed larger than most of the others. Its dark gray skin was rocky and uneven. Yellow puss from necrotic flesh oozed from cracks and mixed with red blood from the fresh wounds that tore open when it moved. She shuddered to imagine the agony the monsters must be in from their skin that never stopped growing.

Chad kept his rifle trained on the beast. He knew if he fired, the others would come rushing in. He hoped that it wouldn't wander in and go somewhere else. He didn't think he had ever seen one so large. It was almost seven foot tall. Maybe taller. The rest was typical of the ragers. Its head seemed small and gaunt with over sized jagged teeth from mineral build up. The monster's muscles bulged and flexed as it moved, even under the massive amounts of dead necrotic tissue that covered its body. It had ripped out of its clothes long ago, wearing nothing more than dark brown ripped underwear that hung loose like a loin cloth in the front. The elastic band had stretched tight around the monster's waist and had become embedded in the rager's skin.

Chad slowly depressed the trigger, but he let off when the monster wandered into the adjacent room to them. He gave a quick glance below them. They were about thirty feet off of the ground. He looked out into the dark tree line. He was pretty sure he would be able to escape into the darkness, but Katie would not be. His thoughts went back to the problem at hand. He kept his rifle trained to the stairs when a second rager approached the doorway. "Katie, we have to take a shot. We can't let them build up."

"Okay, Dad."

Chad took a deep breath and let his bullet fly. The muzzle of the rifle flashed around the broken and crumbled bricks. The beast's head erupted in an explosion of blood and brain matter. It collapsed to the ground in front of the stairs. He took a quick breath and waited for the larger one to come rushing through the door. But, to his surprise, it did not. He could hear growls of the others as they scrambled up the stairs to the sound of his rifle. "I expect the big one to come any minute."

"I'm ready." Katie said through gritted teeth. She was excited to be able to fire her weapon.

"Here they come."

The first rager came up the stairs, its muscles flexing and its thick powerful chest was heaving. She took her first shot. Three cracks and a light muzzle flash lit up the room. The hot lead tore into the neck, jaw, and the side of the monster's head. It erupted in a splash of blood, skull, and brain.

The second beast burst through the door with several other's behind it. Chad fired his three round burst, dropping it. Their turn firing worked like a rhythmic dance, increasing pace as more and more filled the room. They fell in sequence. Each shot hitting its mark and felling the large beasts. But, still they neared.

"Get ready to jump!" Chad growled, knowing Katie had just fired her last three round burst. "Now!"

The father and daughter duo leapt backward, high above the dry Texas ground. Their ropes went taught and they slowly descended down into safety. Their hard boots grabbed tightly against the crumbling tan brick surface. Katie clipped her empty rifle to her harness and transitioned to her shotgun. She was the most comfortable with it in her hands.

"You're empty, right?" Chad checked his ammo.

"Yup." Katie's shotgun erupted, sending several hot pieces of double ought buck into the face of a rager peering over the ledge. Bits of blood and brain rained down on them. "I have twenty five, well now twenty four twelves left."

Chad wiped drops of gore from his face, "Be careful not to get any of their blood in your mouth or in your eyes. If their infection is blood borne, then we can catch it this way."

Another rager poked its head over the side and growled when the beast saw them hanging over the side. Katie raised her shotgun to fire and Chad placed his hand over it. "No, don't shoot."

"Why?"

"Let's not risk getting any more of their blood on us."

Katie bit her lip. "Well, we can't just sit here all night."

"Yea, and it's not like they're going to give up."

Chad gave a quick glance below. There were two empty window slots on either side of them. "Hey, let me go down a level. I might be able to draw some attention and pick a few off on the second level. I've still got thirty two ARs left."

"Okay, Dad."

Chad eased himself down on his repel line. He didn't see any of the monsters on the second floor. He tapped the bricks with his hard soled combat boots and slid to the right. He carefully grabbed the crumbing brick and climbed into the window seal, letting some slack in his safety line. "Looks clear here."

Katie gave a quick glance. Her father was fully in the window. Do you want me to come down, Dad?"

Several ragers erupted from the doorway and rushed the window. Chad raised his rifle to his shoulder and let it go. He did not have time to fire burst shots. Hot lead poured from his barrel and the muzzle flashes lit up the barren second floor like a strobe light. The beasts fell one after another, but they closed the gap on the room. The resounding ping of an empty chamber chimed out from Chad's rifle. He jumped back out of the window just as one of the beasts reached for him.

"Dad!" Katie screamed when the monster reached out of the window.

Chad's momentum took him sideways out and down

between floors. He tried to catch himself with his feet, but the line twisted and his back bounced off of the crumbling brown brick. Like a pendulum, he started to swing back toward the window—toward the growling snarling arms of the gray skinned rager.

Katie lifted her shotgun to her shoulder and squeezed off a round. The buck tore into the monsters head. The beast howled and grabbed its face and fell back inside. She turned her barrel to the beast above her and squeezed of another round, tearing through the monster's head and killing it. It fell forward between the twisted rebar. Its head dripped blood and brain matter like a chunky flow of watery syrup that leaked down the side of the building. Katie tucked her shotgun under her arm and lowered herself down to the window below.

Chad stumbled to get his footing. His rope had let out and he was just under the second floor. Katie lowered herself down to the second story in hopes of providing her father with cover file. She eased out her line, but the window still had glass in it. The glass was old and aged with crisscrossing chicken wire holding it together. Katie put her shotgun in the holster on her back and gripped the brick window sill. She let out her line and climbed onto the ledge. "Dad!"

Chad regained his footing, "Katie. Get out of the window. There is still one—"

The window erupted outward. Powerful muscular gray skinned arms wrapped around the jagged and torn glass, pinning it between Katie and its fetid body. They tumbled back. The force of the blow struck Katie so hard, it took the wind from her lungs. She felt herself harness jerk tight, then snap before the crushing weight of the ground came up to meet her. Sharp stabbing pain erupted from her hips to her shoulders. The gray skinned monster was on top of the glass, pinning her to the ground. It clawed and snarled as it tried to reach her from under the splintered window.

"No!" Chad screamed helplessly. He climbed up into the window and drew his pistol. He took aim, but if he missed the flailing, he would hit Katie for sure.

"Dad!" Katie cried weakly. Her voice cracked and tears filled her eyes. She could not move, pinned under the massive weight of the monster that snarled and growled over her.

Chad lowered himself as fast as he could. He smashed into the ground and lost his footing. Katie's cries and screams awoke a hatred he had never felt. Pulling his knife, Chad cut the rope line and rushed the hulking behemoth, firing with his pistol. His boots tossed up dry dusty earth with each step. His knuckles went white gripping the knife and hot lead tore through the monster's body and shoulder. He neared the monster and with a primal yell, crashed into its hulking body, knocking it from the glass, and stabbing into the monster's neck.

Hot red blood erupted from the wound. The beast backhanded Chad, effortlessly lifting him from the ground and hurling him into the air. Chad struck a small treelike bush. His pistol flew from his hand and he fell to the ground. The rager ignored the spraying blood and charged Chad. He managed to get to his feet as the monster reached him. The beast slammed a heavy fist into his shoulder, knocking Chad from his feet and onto his back.

Katie cried. Tears streaked down her smooth dirty cheeks. She could hear her father fighting for her life—for his life. Ignoring the searing hot stabbing pain of her broken bones, she slid the shattered glass off of her and drew her pistol. She took aim through watery tear filled eyes and squeezed the trigger.

Chad couldn't move his shoulder. He was stunned and laying on his back while the monster stood over him. He knew he needed to move, to get up, to fight—but he couldn't seem to get his body to obey him.

Hot lead tore through the back of the rager. It turned and snarled at Katie while one of her rounds struck it in the knee. The beast growled and limped toward her. Saliva dripped from its taught lipped mouth. Katie emptied her pistol into the monster, yet it continued to limp toward her. "Daddy..." she weakly pleaded through a tearful cracked voice.

Chad suddenly gathered his wits. The sound of his baby girl in pain sent adrenaline and unbridled rage coursing through him. He rushed the rager and leaped onto its back. Wrapping his legs around the thing's waist, he grabbed the monster's hair with his injured hand and stabbed into its neck.

It howled in pain and thrashed about, trying to rip Chad from its shoulders. Chad stabbed again, and again, until finally making deep cuts into the weakening monster's throat. The beast fell face forward, unconscious from bloodloss—and Chad kept cutting. In moments he hoisted the dripping bloody head of the rager by its hair. He screamed at its lifeless face before tossing the head into the darkness.

"Dad, I'm hurt."

Chad rushed to her, his left arm dangling useless at his side. "Just be still."

Katie laid back on the cool Texas earth. She stared up at the dark blue sky that was lightening by the moment from the rising morning sun. Her vision clouded and all went dark.

Chad carefully opened her tactical vest and cut her shirt open. He gently pressed his hand around her ribs and shoulder. He didn't see any bite marks on her body, but he was certain she had at least some broken ribs. He gathered up their firearms and sat on point, guarding the most important person in his life—his injured daughter.

"And there came out of the smoke locusts upon the earth: and unto them was given power, as the scorpions of the earth have power. And it was commanded them that they should not hurt the grass of the earth, neither any green thing, neither any tree; but only those men which have not the seal of God in their foreheads. And to them it was given that they should not kill them, but that they should be tormented five months: and their torment was as the torment of a scorpion, when he striketh a man. And in those days shall men seek death, and shall not find it; and shall desire to die, and death shall flee from them."

Revelation 9:3-6

4
THE PURGE

"What do you mean, they're gone?" Joe slammed his fist down on the counter.

"Joe, they're gone. Scout-1, Scout-2, Warthog, most of the vehicles."

"Where are they going? Springfield?"

"Seems that away." Trina handed him a clip board. "They have Sammy and George."

Joe shook his head in disgust. "Well, radio Springfield and let them know they're coming. It's their problem now."

"What about the USS Typhoon?"

"Send some crews out and begin salvaging the parts from it."

"I'll grab a crew and some vehicles."

Justin sat on a large warm rock and dabbed his feet in the cool river water. His pants legs were rolled to just under his knees and he nonchalantly held his fishing pole with both hands. It has been a long time since he had a full day off to do some fishing. He glanced over at Rikki. The dark haired Philippine held his hand aloft and watched an overly large praying mantis climb up his wrist.

"Dude, that thing's huge." Justin's eyes went wide. "That

would be great fish bait."

"Not a chance."

"But, dude. Man. We could catch the granddaddy with that one."

Rikki ignored Justin and watched the mantis clime up his wrist toward the top of his hand. It was different from the mantis's he remembered. Aside from being the size of a small bird, it had longer wings and larger mandibles. There was an odd barbed end on its abdomen. "Looks like it could sting."

"Praying Mantis don't sting, man."

Rikki frowned and examined it. Then he flicked it quickly from his hand. "Whoa!" The bug took flight and flew across the river to the trees on the far side.

Justin jumped, "What?!"

"Do you think it had the virus in it?"

Justin laughed, "No way. It looked like a mnntis to me."

"Yeah, but it had a weird stinger thing."

"Mantises don't have stingers. They have claws and everything, but no stingers."

"This one had something on it."

Justin plopped down and shook his head, "You just flipped away good fish bait."

"Well, the next demon bug that lands on your hand, you can kill it."

Justin laughed and cast his line back in the water. The plastic lure went errant and got caught in a small Texas overhang tree limb. "Fuck."

Rikki laughed, "See, them devil bugs have powers."

Justin stood up and dusted himself off while holding on to his pole. He lightly tugged. The line went taught and the branch slowly bent down under the pressure. "Dammit."

"It's up there, good."

Justin pulled the pole straight down. The plastic line stretched.

"You're going to snap the line. That stuff is like gold."

"It'll be fine."

"Dude, it's gonna snap. Just shake it out."

Justin groaned, handing Rikki the pole, "You get it unsnagged then."

Rikki bit his lip. Grabbing the pole he gave it several quick and violent jerks back and forth. Leaves fell from the branch. "Man, it's in there good."

A sharp pain hit Justin in the back of the neck. "Fuck!" He swatted and jumped.

Rikki stood confused. "What'er you doing?"

"Something stung me."

Rikki laughed, and gave the pole a final violent shake. Dozens of large green mantises fell from the branch. Rikki ducked and raised his arms. He cried out in pain as they stung him, slapping his hands on his body, killing a few. The other's took flight and flew to other trees. "They fucking stung me!"

Justin laughed, gently rubbing the back of his neck. "They prolly bit you. I'm telling you a mantis can't sting."

Rickki motioned to large red bumps on his arms and his cheek. "Oh yeah? What the fuck do you call these?"

"Bites?"

"Whatever it is, it fucking hurts. I'm going in."

Justin chuckled, "What about the pole?"

"Leave the damn pole. We can get it later."

Justin rubbed his neck and glanced at the pole. It hung from the tree and gently swayed back and forth. He called out to Rikki as he jogged to catch up, "I don't think that pole is coming down anytime soon, man."

The pair walked into medical. Rikki stumbled and leaned against the door frame. His dark face seemed pale and he was sweating profusely.

"What's wrong guys?" Marty walked towards them. The sizeable man's long curly brown hair hung loosely about the shoulders of his white lab coat.

"We got stung by a swarm of praying mantises," Rikki mumbled.

"Mantises don't sting, guys. Go down to the garage and see what the problem is."

"I think I might pass out." Rikki leaned his hot head against the cold metal door frame.

"Let me have a quick look," Marty lifted his glasses from his pocket to his eyes. "You have a lot of spots here. They do look like stings. Are you sure these were mantises and not ground hornets?"

Justin nodded, rubbing his neck, "Yup. I saw it. Damndest thing. It looked like a mantis, but it was bigger and had a long stinger thing on its butt thingy."

"Doesn't sound like a mantis at all."

Marty frowned, "Take him over to the table. Get his shirt off."

Justin helped Rikki to the table and took off his shirt. His body was covered in dozens thick red welts about the size of quarters. "Damn, Marty. He's pretty messed up."

Marty walked over and flipped on the light that hung over the examination table. He started pushing and probing on the welts.

"Whatcha' doin'?"

"Looking to see if there was a stinger left in, or if there is any venom."

Justin glanced around the room. "Say, where is Sammy?"

Marty did not look up, "She left with a few others to head up to Springfield, MO headquarters to get her to their medical lab."

"What kind of a lab do they have?"

"No clue, I've never been there," Marty reached for a cotton swab, "But, since ZOD had a strong network of fans and geeks—seems there were several doctors in that area that brought their medical supplies and expertise there and opened a lab."

Justin grimaced, "Gross. Is that puss?"

Marty dabbed the swab in a yellowish fluid that he squeezed out of one of the red welts. "Not sure. I doubt it's puss. Most likely, some sort of venom."

Justin leaned over. "Nah, man. Look at that stuff. Looks like it has some sort of pudding stuff in it."

Marty dabbed some of the puss with a cotton swab and put it on a glass slide. He took it over to one of their small mirrored microscopes. He flipped on the light and adjusted the settings. Justin Hovered over.

"What do ya' see?"

"Oh, this doesn't seem good."

"Yeah, I think Rikki passed out."

"No, I mean this fluid."

THE APOCALYPSE OF ENOCH

Justin rubbed his bald head. "What about it?"

Marty stood up and turned to face him. "Those little clear nodules you thought looked like tapioca..."

"Yeah?"

Marty's face went stone cold. "They're eggs. And there are dozens on this swab alone."

Justin turned back to Rikki. "Oh man, he's fucked."

"Good morning, Katie bug." Chad poured a steamy pot of coffee into a small tin cup.

Katie smiled, "I hurt all over."

"Here," Chad handed her the tin cup. "Drink this."

Katie frowned, "Coffee? Dad I hate coffee."

"Well, I thought you might like some pep. We can't stay here long. We need to get back to the gas station."

Katie sipped the coffee. She didn't much care for the taste, but something other than the bland flavor of water was a welcome sensation. "Can we take the road back?"

"You mean head back south?"

Kaite shook her head and held the coffee in both hands. "No, I saw a road to the west this morning when I was waiting for the monsters to come up the stairs."

"Are you sure?"

"Yup." It ran north and south."

Chad filled his small tin cup with the remaining bit of coffee. "Well, going west isn't exactly the same direction we wanted to go, but we can."

Katie grimaced and got to her feet. "The thought of going up and down a few hills makes me want to cry."

"Okay, kiddo." Chad got to his feet and rubbed her hair, messing it up. "I gathered up our firearms. You use your Benelli. I'm going to need to use some of your forty rounds."

"Okay, Dad." Katie grimaced and got to her feet. "I hurt all over."

"Well, I think you have broken ribs. I don't want you

moving much. If you start bleeding inside it can kill you."

Katie paused, worry in her eyes, "Aren't you supposed to say something uplifting or encouraging?"

"Well, ..." Chad rubbed his chin. "How about, don't move around too much and stab one of your broken ribs into an organ and you won't die."

Katie smiled, "Thanks, Dad."

"I love you."

"I love you too. Now, let's get moving before more of them ragers come back."

Chad walked slowly so Katie could keep up. The morning sun rose high into the sky and beat down on the dry Texas landscape. They made their way for a little over an hour, stopping often so Katie could rest. When they reached the road, Katie plopped down one a light green plastic electrical box. "My ribs hurt, Dad. Especially when I breath."

"Well, you should have some sort of support—but honestly, Katie—I don't know how tight to tie it and I'm afraid of squeezing your ribs and causing more damage." Chad ignored the burning in his shoulder and the tingling that often shot down to his finger tips.

Katie grimaced and nodded, tenderly holding her hand to her side. "Just let me rest for a bit before we head back."

Wake up. You are ready to serve.

Sammy awoke and rubbed her tired eyes with her shoulder. "Huh?"

Sarah dabbed her forehead. "Morning."

Sammy went to wipe her eyes, but the thick leather restraints held her arms. "Really? Still?"

"We have to take precautions, Sammy."

Artez leaned back, "So, why do they call you Sammy. I thought your name was Integrity. Is that like a code name or something?"

Sammy sat up and looked out the window. "It's my

middle name."

"Wait, your middle name is Integrity?"

"Yup," Sammy nodded.

"That's pretty damn cool."

"Not as cool as not being tied down."

Artez shrugged, "That's their call."

Chris grabbed the mic of his radio, "Hey guys, we have two people on the side of the road up here."

"Scout-2, here. I say we keep going."

"Warthog here, I say stop. We can handle two people."

Chris slowed Scout-1 and pulled to the side of the road before reaching them. It was a man and a woman. They were dressed on combat gear and were well armed. Chris stopped Scout-1 in the middle of the road. He switched his radio to PA. "Sir and ma'am, let me see your hands."

"Jesus," Chad groaned lifting his hands, "He's going to attract a ton monsters with that loud ass radio."

Katie didn't say anything. She struggled to lift her arms and grimaced in pain.

"The girl seems hurt." Artez opened his car door and stood just outside of it. "Hey, what are your names?"

"My name is Chad Francis." Chad kept his hands up, "My daughter and I were attacked last night by ragers. We aren't infected, but I think she has some broken ribs. We are just looking for some bandages or something I can wrap her midsection with."

The righteous are nearing. Hold fast.

Sammy took her gaze from Chad and Katie and frowned, looking at Sarah. "Did you hear that?"

"Yeah, sounded like he said she was injured." Sarah turned to Chris, "Chris, you want me to check them out?"

"Yeah, hold on." Chris picked up the mic again, "I need you to put down your weapons and keep your hands up. I'm going to send out our medical officer." He and Artez drew their rifles and pointed them at the pair.

"Medical officer?" Katie asked weakly.

"Yeah, they have the same markings as that group we met back by the gas station. The ones in the van." Chad placed his firearms on the ground at his feet.

Sarah stepped from the car and cautiously made her way to them. "Hi. Um, my name is Sarah Corso. I'm the chief medical officer for research and development of ZOD for the Texas Division."

Chad smiled, "My name is Chad. This is my daughter Katie. I think she has broken ribs."

Sarah smiled and placed her stethoscope in her ears, "Okay, honey. I'm going to listen to your lungs. Can you breathe like a big girl?"

Katie grimaced as she inhaled, "Sarah—I'm fourteen. Not, four. And I can probably outshoot every single person on your convoy."

Sarah smiled. The kid had spunk, "Okay, well no talking. I need to listen to you breathe."

"Katie, how about you don't piss off the people that can help us?"

"Sorry, Dad."

Sarah lifted the stethoscope and placed it in several different places before taking it from her ears. "Your lungs sounds fine. You have a lot of bruising, so without an x-ray, it would be my guess you have at the very least, bruised ribs. But, let's treat them like they're broke."

"So, do you have a compress, or a wrap or something we can put on her?"

"I think I might have something in our medical bag. Where are you two headed?"

"We're from Jeff City, Missouri area. We were at a three gun tourney here in Texas when shit hit the fan. Trying to make our way back home."

"Three gun?"

"It's a professional competitive shooting event. Rifle, shotgun, pistol."

"Interesting."

"You guys ZOD?" Chad arched an eyebrow.

"Yup. We're taking a patient to the Springfield, Missouri chapter."

"Mind if we tag a long?"

"Let me ask." Sarah walked back to Scout-1. "Chris—"

"I heard. Tell them they have to surrender their weapons

and they can come."

"Sorry." Chad yelled out. "We appreciate your help, but will never surrender our weapons."

"Well, we don't really know you. We can't let you have your weapons."

"I understand." Chad nodded. "No worries."

Artez leaned over, "Chris, the guy is a three gunner. They're almost always cops and former military folks. He is with his daughter. I'm sure he will be fine."

Chris frowned. He reached in his car and flipped the mic back to radio. "Hey, we got two more—skilled shooters—you got room in Scout-2?"

"Yeah, we can squeeze two more."

"This is against my better judgment, but we have room in Scout-2."

"We are much obliged."

Sarah led them past Scout-1. Chad looked inside and saw Sammy secured in the back with the leather restraints. "What's going on with her. She looks like the crack shot we met last week."

"That's Sammy. She was one of our best, but she came down with the virus. She isn't dangerous yet, but we are keeping her in restraints until we get to the medical division."

"Um, it's my experience the infected turn in just a few hours."

"Nah, she has some new strain. Not sure what it will do, but so far she has not changed, shown any signs of being dangerous, and has all her mental faculties."

Chad took a deep breath. He didn't like getting near the infection, but he knew Katie would never be able to make the walk back to the gas station by nightfall and spending a another night in the wilderness with limited ammo would be certain death if they came up on a group of ragers again.

Sarah opened the back door to Scout-2. Chad helped Katie get inside. She groaned with pain before getting settled. He closed the door and extended his hand to Sarah. "Thanks for your help. You may very well have saved our lives by giving us a ride."

"Well, we can take you as far as Springfield."

"That's okay. Jeff City isn't too far north east from there up forty four." Chad, sat down in the rear passenger seat and closed the door.

The driver looked at Chad in the review mirror, "Hey. The names Ratchet." He motioned to the passenger, "this here is Tibbs. He's a rapper."

"Um, hello. I'm Chad, this is my daughter Katie."

Katie tried her best to muster a smile.

Sarah walked up to the passenger side window and motioned for it to be lower. She handed Chad a wide long light tan wrap. "Use this for Katie's ribs. Don't make it very tight. The nature of the wrap should do that."

"Thanks," Chad took the wrap. "I mean it. Thanks for your help."

Sarah just smiled a dorky smile and walked back to Scout-1.

"Nice to have ya' along for the ride." Ratchet slid Scout-2 into drive. The small car crunched the dry rocks from the side of the road before pulling out onto the sun bleached asphalt.

Incessant thumps of heavy barefoot steps echoed on the hot hard asphalt of interstate forty four. His thick muscled chest heaved and labored with each step, but he did not stop or even slow. His bones ached, his muscles burned, but he stopped only to eat. It didn't matter what. A feral human, a squirrel, a cat, even the yappy hairy dog he found trapped in the van.

Once his insatiable hunger had subsided enough to be ignored, he continued his run. Corey wasn't sure what was calling him, but he knew one thing. Nothing was going to stop him from getting there. Ideas were hard now. Numbers were things he once knew. Words were now more akin to thoughts expressed through grunts and sounds. He was making good time. It wouldn't be long before he would be able to answer the call that tugged at his soul.

THE APOCALYPSE OF ENOCH

"And the four angels were loosed, which were prepared for an hour, and a day, and a month, and a year, for to slay the third part of men."

Rev 9:15

5
DELIVER ME WITH EVIL

"This is bullshit." Sammy growled. "Virus or not, I'm not crazy, I'm not biting anyone, or any of that other stupid shit."

"We can't take any chances," Sarah slid a lock of her long brown hair behind her ear. "That's why we're taking you to Springfield, to the medical division."

"If I had herpes you wouldn't tie me up."

"This is far worse than that."

"She has a point, Sarah." Artez looked back, holding onto the handle above the passenger side window. "I mean, even if she had ebola—would we tie her up?"

"Well, she would be isolated."

"Okay, so isolated but not tied up."

"I'm not a fucking prisoner. I'm the best sniper you have."

"I just want to be safe, Sammy. No one knows how this stuff works. And your virus..."

"What? What about it?"

"Sammy, it was nothing like I had ever seen before. Aside from the bioluminescence—which was cool—it was binding to your chromosomes."

"Huh?" Artez looked back. "I thought viruses attacked cells."

Sarah sighed,"Well, yes. It's complicated. The strain Sammy has does attack cells, but instead of converting the T-cell like it has in every other infected person we have seen, this one is binding to it... and changing it."

"Changing it how?" Sammy asked with interest.

"Well, each cell has two sets of sex chromosomes. They are pretty much inactive in all somatic cells."

"Huh?" Artez groaned. "Dumb cop terms, please."

"It is giving off the typical enzyme—but doing it by attaching to the double X. Meaning, I think it's only contagious to women."

"Great, we get periods, cramps, and now our very own zombie virus." Sammy shook her head and stared out the window.

"Well, maybe. I don't know. Joe ordered you and George to be terminated before I could do many tests. And, I'm not exactly a molecular biologist or anything. I'm more of a pharmacist. That's why I want to take you to Springfield. Maybe this is as far of a change as you will go."

Sammy turned back to Sarah. "I'm not letting you kill me."

"No one is—"

"You have me tied up. You're keeping me. You haven't asked if I want a cure. You haven't asked me a damned thing."

"Well, we don't know if you're going to turn dangerous."

Sammy narrowed her eyes. "Oh, I'm dangerous. And I'll humor your little restraints. But, if you move to harm me, I'll kill everyone in this car."

"Whoa, hold on now." Artez laughed. "I didn't do shit. I just came along for the ride."

"Then set me free. If you're not fighting my captors, you're one of them."

"Sarah, this chic is creeping me out."

Sammy turned her head and looked out the backseat window again. "You all have been warned."

"If you're done planning everyone's doom, there is a gas station ahead." Chris gestured down the road. "I'm going to call out."

Artez didn't say anything. Chris looked in the rearview mirror. Sammy was looking out of the window and Sarah shrugged. Chris picked up the mic, "Gas station ahead."

"Scout-2, let's stop."

"Warthog here, let's stop."

"10-4," Chris slowed and turned into the rock parking

lot. Bodies were lying outside and half in and half out of the windows. They were bloated and rotting in the hot Texas sun.

"Warthog to Scout-1 it looks like something went down here not too long ago."

Chris stopped his car next to a large silver propane tank. He and Artez got out and drew their rifles. They approached the first corpse. Chris nudged it with his foot. "Looks like it took one to the head."

Artez nodded. "So did these. I'm guessing some folks were holed up here."

"You think there are any survivors?"

Artez shrugged, "I'm more interested in supplies."

Chris went back to his car and picked up the mic, "Send me two more to go with Artez to sweep the inside to look for supplies."

"Warthog here. Sending Tibbs and Nettleton."

"10-4." Chris stood back out from the car. "You okay sweeping it?"

Artez nodded. "Yea, Nettleton and I are probably the most qualified. He did it in Iraq and I did it all the time as a member of the tactical team in Saint Louis."

Chris nodded, "What about Tibbs?"

Tibbs walked by and chuckled, "Shit, Brolo. I'm a gangsta. I can handle anything."

Shane laughed, "We're okay, Chris. Just have the cars ready to go in the event we come out screaming like little girls with some baddies on our six."

The trio made their way around the front. Dead bodies littered the outside and hanging inside the windows. Small piece of furniture were jammed behind boards and other things tacked up to barricade them.

"Looks like someone was living here before they were bummed rushed." Tibbs pointed at the boards. "Those were tacked on from the outside."

"Well, at least the good guys won." Shane motioned around the side.

Artez and Tibbs rounded the corner to see a small dirt grave with a make shift grave stone. "Well, maybe. That could have happened before. Let's still be careful."

Tibbs stared at the grave. His thoughts lingered on the person's death. He thought of Jeff. He thought of Nish.

"Tibbs?"

"Huh?"

"We're heading in." Shane ripped open the door to star into the red bloodshot eyes of a feral. It was leaning over the bloated body of what appeared to be another dead feral. Blood and rotted flesh dripped from its mouth. Shane squeezed the trigger on his rifle, sending a single shot into the monster's face. The back of its head erupted and the beast collapsed silently.

"Oh shit." Tibbs laughed. "It was eating the dick of the dead one."

"Huh?" Artez advanced into the room, scanning for any other movement. Shane moved to the north wall, keeping his rifle trained on the door that he suspected went to the lobby.

Tibbs kicked the recently killed feral over and pointed down to the body it was eating, "Look. It was eating the crotch of the other dead feral. Now that's some funny shit."

"Seriously?" Artez turned his attention to the body. "Sure as fuck was. Shane, check that out."

Shane moved to the door to the lobby,"Let's stay on task gentleman."

"I'm just sayin' we don't get much humor anymore. And a dick eating zombie is some funny shit." Tibbs laughed.

"Wait, look and see if it had a wallet or something. We must remember this dick eating zombie for all time." Artez laughed.

Tibbs chuckled and flipped the body over. He ignored the stench of the purtrifacting corpses in the small hot room. He stood up quickly and held a wallet in the air, placing his other hand on his hip. "We have walletification!"

"Goddamn it, you two."Shane growled. "We have another fucking door to check."

The pair continued undaunted. "Dear Tibbsy, would you be so kind as to discover the identity of our dick eating friend?"

"Why, I would be honored to." Tibbs playfully opened the wallet, removed a driver's license, and tossed the wallet in the corner of the room in an exaggerated motion. He lifted the license to his face, "And our winner is, ...Brandon Cunningham."

Artez burst out in laughter. "Cunningham? Check his teeth? Cause if they're fucked up he must be English!"

Tibbs scrunched his nose, "Gross. You check em."

"Okay, are you done? I'd really like to get out of this fucking oven."

"Fine, fine." Artez chuckled and raised his rifle to his shoulder. "Ready."

Shane flipped open the door to the lobby. The smell of rotting flesh erupted from the room and washed over them. Shane choked and fought the urge to gag.

"Amateur." Artez pushed past him and checked the room, "Clear."

Shane covered his mouth and went in. The entire room was a mass of rotting bodies and flies. He quickly backed out of the room, coughing.

Tibbs stepped in, "It can't be that—holy hell." Tibbs gagged and coughed. He ran back into the garage. "Holy hell!"

Shane wiped tears from his eyes and gathered his composure. "Anything of value in there, Artez?"

Artez came out shaking his head. "Nothing we want to try and salvage. Between the heat and the rotting—everything in there is shit."

"Well, let's grab some supplies and tools from the garage here." Shane walked from the garage and took a deep breath from the fresh hot air.

Tibbs followed Artez out, "So, why didn't that smell bother you?"

"When you're a cop in Saint Louis, you get used to rotting bodies."

Shane waved to Scout-1 and the others. They came out and they started loading up supplies into the trunks of the vehicles. Chris wiped sweat from his brow, keeping on hand on the waistline of his pants. "Any belts in there?"

Shane shrugged, "Maybe. The apocalypse diet cutting weight off of you?"

"Yeah. I should have came up with this before everything went to shit. Coulda' made a ton of money."

"Any belts in there?" Shane grabbed a thick plastic milk crate full of tools.

Tibbs walked by with a long copper wire coiled into a five gallon bucket. There were wires coming off of it that had clamps like a car battery clamp.

Chris looked at the wires. "That might make a belt."

"I don't know. It looks important to me. The wires were sitting in the bucket that was full of water and the other end was attached to some car batteries."

"Car batteries?"

"Yeah, like forty of them in there. All got charges too. This place is the mother lode."

Shane set his crate down and started pointing to parts on the wire, "That my friends, is a Tesla coil."

"Like a radio?" Tibbs wiped the sweat from his cheek on his shoulder.

"No, when charged, it produces ozone."

"Sounds sketchy."

"So what does the ozone do?" Chris glanced around the other tools that were being stacked at the rear of the vehicles. "Besides NOT make a belt?"

"Well, it does a lot—but when stuck into a bucket of water—it would kill bacteria and stuff. So, that my friends, was most likely being used as a water purification device."

"Put that in the Warthog. More room and it could be useful."

Tibbs nodded and took the bucket and wire system back toward the SUV.

"This was where Katie and I were staying," Chad walked up, rubbing his sore shoulder. "There should have been two others. Steve Zehner and Ashlee Madix."

Shane frowned, "Sorry. There isn't anyone inside that is alive. We found a grave outback."

"There wasn't a grave when we left a few days ago. So, one of them survived and fled."

"Maybe we will find them on the road. But, we can't go looking for them. No time."

Chad bit his lip, "Not a big deal. They weren't family. Hell, they were barely friends. Not that I wish ill on them. But, I'm not interested in staying out here on the road to find them."

"Fair enough."

Chad started back to the Warthog before pausing, "They

were good people, though. Steve was a corrections officer, or a cop, or something. Ashlee was a school teacher."
"Well, say a prayer for them if you're into that kind of thing."
Chad stared off for a moment and then walked back.

THE APOCALYPSE OF ENOCH

"And when they shall have finished their testimony, the beast that ascendeth out of the bottomless pit shall make war against them, and shall overcome them, and kill them."

Rev 11:7

6
THE MANTIS QUEEN COMETH

"Joe, wake up."

He opened his eyes and saw Ricky. The once overweight ZOD member was almost unrecognizable from his weight loss.

"What time is it?"

"Noonish."

Joe sat up and rubbed his eyes from the long night. "Did we ever get in contact with the Springfield Chapter?"

"We have more pressing problems." The messenger seemed distressed.

"What now?" Joe got up from his bunk and wetted his toothbrush. "Like we ran out of toothpaste? That was a month ago."

"No, I mean that zealots are back."

Joe bent over the sink and vigorously scrubbed his teeth, rinsing and spitting. "Christ, what do they want now?"

"Um... they are demanding our surrender and repentance."

"What?" Joe stood up. His toothbrush hung loosely from his mouth.

"There are over a thousand of them, Sir. They are giving us thirty minutes and then they're coming in—or so they say."

Joe dressed hurriedly. "That's insane. Do they all have guns?"

"I'm not sure, Sir. They are requesting to speak with you."

Joe placed his foot on the small stool and laced up his black combat boots. "I've about had it with these fuck holes."

"What should I tell everyone?"

"Tell them to be ready to defend our complex. I'll go out to meet them as soon as I'm dressed."

The watch nodded and left the room. Joe buttoned up his black shirt. It was faded from the sun, but still had a strong presence to it. He grabbed his hat and walked from his room.

The cool hallway was abuzz with ZOD members running to their perspective positions. He knew they had never defended the complex against thinking people before. Joe then laughed. He just referred to religious zealots as thinking people.

"Joe, they are out front again." Ricky said, nervously gripping his rifle.

Joe tucked his shirt into his loose fitting pants. The apocalypse diet has really cut a ton of weight off. He clipped his gun belt on and walked up the stairs to the front door. "I'm sure these yay-whos will just go away and pray to their fake god some more."

"I don't know, Sir. They seem pretty serious this time."

Joe squinted and raised his hand to his eyes to shield them from the sun. There were dozens of vehicles parked out front of the chain link fence. He quickly spied the crazy old man standing on top of the white truck leading prayer over a mega phone. "Well, they sure can put on a show."

"Yes, they can." Ricky pointed to the east. "If you look over there, you can see they have hundreds lining the river on the other side."

Joe casually walked down the driveway from the parking lot to the gate. He squinted his left eye to the eastern sun. "Do they have guns?"

"I don't think so, Sir. But, they have clubs, pipes, and some have swords."

Joe, chuckled. "Swords?"

"Yes, Sir."

"Nebuchadnezzar, what do you want now?" Joe asked, grabbing the chain link fence and leaning against it.

"...and may the Lord protect us with his righteous might, Amen." The old man finished praying over the megaphone. He let it drop nonchalantly to his side. "Your ZOD group is—"

"Yeah, yeah, Neb. I know. We're evil and all that. Look,

what do you want now?"

"I demand that you repent and allow those in your den of wickedness that wish to find the glory of God and receive his salvation to come out and humble their selves before me."

"Yeah, that's not gonna' happen. Anything else?"

He shook his head, "Then you have doomed your people."

"Right, seems like we are living just fine, Neb. So, how about you take your cult back across the bridge and leave us alone?"

The old man raised up his megaphone. His long white beard shook in the light breeze. "There is a price to pay for being the leader of men!"

"Psh." Joe waved his hand and dismissed the zealots. He turned and started walking back to the compound when a single shot echoed across the dry Texas land. Joe felt a hard punch in his back. It stole his breath. "I—" Blood erupted from his mouth and poured down his chin. He struggled to breathe.

"Joe!" Ricky grabbed his shoulder and tried to hold him up.

"In the name of our Lord God, we will cleanse the land of these heathenish monsters that have brought this curse upon us!"

Joe fell face down onto the roadway. A second shot rang out, clipping Ricky in the side of the head. Blood and gore erupted from the wound and he crumbled next to Joe.

In a tidal wave of white, the rusted vehicles rushed forward, tearing through the chain link fence.

"They shot Joe!" Justin raised his rifle to his shoulder and started firing.

Gun fire erupted from the complex. Heavy lead rounds thumped against the white vehicles. The zealots tore through the chain fence. The thin metal barricade clanged as the vehicles tore through it and powered across the tall grass toward the complex.

Pete peered out from a second story window overlooking

the rover. Hundreds of men dressed in white splashing into the water. They carried bats and swords. A few had firearms, but they took aim and fired from the shore and did not advance. Pete raised his rifle to his shoulder and fired. Dirt erupted at the feet of one of the sword wielding men. He ducked and moved over a few feet and reset to fire again.

Pete took aim a second time and squeezed the trigger. The man in white hunched over forward grabbing the wound in his chest. He tumbled down the dry embankment in a trail of dust before splashing into the river.

"Shoot the swimmers" a voice shouted near Pete. "There are too many to let them reach the shore."

Pete turned his rifle toward the splashing men, swimming and wading with their weapons in their hands. His rifle shook against his shoulder and the man sunk beneath the waves. Pete grimaced from the pain in his chest. He wasn't fully healed yet. In moments, he shook off the pain and fired again and again. Dozens of men had sunk beneath the surface from his shots, but there were so many, they were reaching the shore.

Pete raised his rifle and paused. What had happened to the world? How was it possible that after this plague had hit and ended civilization, people were still willing to fight and try to kill others? It made no sense. Pete squeezed the trigger. His rifle shook lightly as another man fell over.

They came out of the river in droves. Their white sheets were soaked and heavy, making them off balance as they climbed out of the river. Round after round tore into the men, cutting them down—but they continued to charge. They rushed the doors and windows. Shot after shot dropped more and more, but there was too many. When they breached the lower levels Pete began to get concerned. Was he going to survive this long only to be killed by crazy nutjobs in white robes?

The large white truck slammed into the double doors of the complex. Glass shattered and the metal door frame twisted and bent under the force of the blow. Vehicle after vehicle slammed into the walls of the building. Most of them were unable to breach the walls, leaving their occupants bloody and dazed inside their cars and trucks. Gun fire still erupted from the ground floors and second stories, but the men continued undaunted.

Trina raised up from behind the desk in the front lobby. She squeezed the trigger of her rifle. The weapon sprang to life. Hot lead ripped through the first three men through the front lobby. The zealots responded with gun fire. She ducked low, ignoring the sharp pain that punched into her shin and left forearm. She went to stand to return fire, but her leg gave out from under her. She fell to the side. She started to raise her weapon up, but a close range shotgun blast silenced her.

The men rushed the lobby, killing the four other ZOD members. Gun fire occasionally sounded down the hallway into the lobby, but the zealots kept pouring in and filling the complex.

"Our Lord God hath delivered us into the belly of the beast! Let his strength give us glory in our righteous might!"

The men shouted Amen before rushing down the hallway to be gunned down. They ran with their hands outstretched in front of them and heads down. Hot lead ripped through their bodies and they fell, only to be replaced by the second wave, and then the third, until they tackled the ZOD defenders and beat them to death in the hall.

"They're in!" Steph yelled. "She kneeled outside the doorway with her rifle on her shoulder.

Sinjin wiped a lock of his curly red sweaty hair from his face. "Oh fuck, oh fuck."

"Just be calm and fall back towards the stairs."

The pair could hear the screams and shrieks as their fellow ZOD members were cut down and beat to death in the other rooms.

"I think we need to bail." Sinjin's nervous voice cracked.

"Bail where?"

"We have vehicles here."

Steph bit her lip. "If we took the medical bay ladder to the second floor, we might be able to get there."

Sinjin hopped up and ran back down the hall.

"Well, shit." Steph groaned. She wasn't the tuck and run type, but it didn't sound like the battle was going the way she would have liked.

Sinjin burst into the medical room. He slung his rifle over his back, he hurried up the ladder to the ceiling in the far backside of the room. Steph jerked open cabinets and stuffed her pouches and pockets with medical supplies.

"Come on!"

Steph grabbed one more handful and crammed them down her shirt before grabbing the ladder. She could hear more gunfire and shouts and screams coming from down the hall. Steph climbed to the top and pulled herself through the hatch. She had lost quite a bit of weight since everything fell apart. "How about that?"

Sinjin smiled nervously, "Yeah, could have used that during the Mudder Race in Saint Louis last year."

Steph dusted herself off and closed the hatch before locking it. "Ha! You spend most of the time whining about how cold it was."

Sinjin fumbled around the wall looking for a light switch. "It was cold."

"It was like 60 degrees—at least."

"And windy." Sinjin corrected, before turning the door handle. It opened into an upstairs hall. He could hear gun fire.

Steph moved up behind him and checked her weapon one more time to make sure it would fire if she needed it to. The pair made their way down the hall.

"Fuck this."

Sinjin poked his head around the corner. "Pete!"

Pete slung his rifle over his shoulder. "Too goddammed many of them. We need to bail."

Steph nodded, "We're headed to the garage to snag a vehicle."

"Sounds great!" Pete smiled and rubbed his side.

They made their way down the hall to the tight metal spiral stair case that led to the garage. Sinjin and Steph entered slowly with their weapons raised. Pete paused at the top of the iron stairwell. "I'll cover ya'."

Steph went around the north side of the garage and Sinjin went around the south side, meeting at the garage doors. Sinjin grabbed a set of keys "Wrangler 2!"

"Hell yeah!" Steph shouted and jumped into the passenger side of the jeep. "Just like the old ZERV we had back in Saint Louis."

Sinjin hit the green garage door button and jumped in the driver's seat. He turned the ignition and Pete jumped in the back.

"Hold on!" Sinjin yelled and popped the clutch on the jeep. It rocketed to life and shot out of the garage. The top of the roll bars clipped the bottom of the garage door. Bits of plastic and rubber ripped loose as the Jeep shot up the concrete ramp. Cranking the wheel hard right, they turned onto the road to the north, amid the growingly distant gunfire from the complex.

"There are nine captured heathens left."

The man rubbed his hands on his long white robes. They were blood stained around the cuffs and on his thighs from wiping his bloody hands on them. "I'm tired of purging their souls today."

"So, put them off for tomorrow?"

"No, our God is a vengeful God. We offered them a chance to repent. They hardened their hearts."

"Shoot them?"

"No, of course not. Through pain may they be forced to reconcile with our Lord. This may take several days."

"But, we need to get back to our town. Our gardens need tending. We need to—"

"I know what we need to do, Harold." The man in white wiped took a pitcher of water and doused it on his hands and washed away the excess blood. "Crucify them. If they do not appreciate the sacrifice Jesus made for them, maybe they will figure out when they are up on a cross."

"It will be done."

Tori grimaced at the bloody wound in her leg. It was deep and she had lost a lot of blood. Her toes tingled and her foot was going numb. She struggled against the duct tape that bound her hands behind her, but she was unable to break it.

"You did good, T3-ZD." Rich sad sadly. The robot lay on its side, broken. Exposed wires littered the floor and dozens and dozens of gunshot dents covered its armored body.

"Shut up!" The man in white smashed the butt of his shotgun stock into Rich's face. "Thou shall not worship a graven image!"

Rich fell over. Blood streamed from the fresh cut on his eyebrow and pooled into the strained and scorched office carpet.

"Repent, heathen!" The man yelled at Rich before kicking him in the ribs.

"Leave him alone!"

The man grabbed Tori by her hair and jerked her head up to his. His fetid breath poured out from between his clenched teeth, "You little fucking blasphemous cunt."

Tori winced in a pain.

"Didn't a man ever teach you how to show some respect?"

Harold walked in the room, "Stop wasting your time. These heathens are to be put down."

Tori could hear the others crying and pleading for their lives as she was dragged up the stairs and down the hallway. She grabbed the man's wrist with her good arm to lesson some of the pain of her hair being ripped out of her head. The loud thud of the front doors being kicked open echoed in the hall and the bright afternoon sun flooded over them.

"Ow, he fucking bit me."

Tori didn't open her eyes. The pain from her leg was screaming at her and her injured arm was almost all the way numb. A single gunshot echoed in the hall. The others wailed and shrieked even louder. She opened her eyes to see Rich's lifeless form staring at her. His left eye was bulging and threatening to pop out of its socket from the bullet wound in the side of his face. His chest rose and fell in rapid succession, like a panting dog before the zealot fired a second round into his head. This one ripped Rich's face apart sending a spray of red blood and brain matter over the floor and lower corridor wall. She wanted to cry, to beg, to run, to fight—but her injuries kept her still. She was resigned to her fate.

"So, if we are going to crucify them—where do we get the wood?"

Harold stopped dragging Tori and rubbed his beard with his other hand. "Hmmm, There was some lumber in the garage."

"Yeah, Levi gathered that all up. There's enough for two crosses."

"Well, we need five."

"Well, we aint got five, now do we?"

Harold rubbed his face in frustration, "Just go get the damn wood we got. We'll figure it out from there." He jerked Tori up by her hair and pulled her face close, "See, look at the problems your wicked ways cause."

Tori didn't reply. She took her mind back to another time, before the collapse of the world. She imagined the gym where she worked out. She imagined the beach where she was from. The small town she grew up in. She forced her mind to take her anywhere but where she was—on a dry grassy lawn of an overrun fuel storage hub.

"Now, Dave!" One of the ZOD members shouted.

Tori watched Dave leap to his feet and run.

Harold whirled and raised his shotgun to his shoulder. He squeezed the trigger and it lurched in his arms. Hot buckshot erupted from the barrel and tore into Dave's leg. The other ZOD members jumped up and charged, they had cut the tape that bound them. Harold turned and fired a second shot, hitting one of the men in the face. The other two barreled into Harold, knocking him from his feet.

Fists rained down quickly. Tori fought to bring herself back from her daze.

Get up. I have plans for you.

Tori struggled to her feet. The wound in her leg was

screaming at her. Fresh blood pushed out chunky clots as her muscle flexed. The hot sticky fluid dripped down her leg and she struggled to run to the tree line.

"Dave, are you okay?" Jason started loading his pockets with shotgun shells. His sweaty shaggy brown hair shook and bounced.

Dave shook his head. "That buck tore into me pretty good. I'm going to need some bandages when we get clear."

"How about you, Bob?"

"I'm—"A heavy lead round struck Bob in the shoulder. The force of the high caliber round ripped a giant hole in his chest. The round struck Jason in the arm, grazing him, and leaving a deep gash.

The sound of the gun shot blew past as Bob fell dead.

"Run!" Jason grabbed Tori under her arm and they ran towards the trees.

Gun fire opened behind them. They could hear the heavy lead rounds tearing into the trees in front of them.

As they hit the tree line, they heard Dave fall. The heavy lead bullet thudded into his back like a heavy punch. Dave gasped and fell, but they didn't dare turn around.

Jason ran with his legs high, trying to step over the underbrush. Tori struggled to just move forward, ignoring the stinging pain as the thorns drug across her skin, ripping it open.

"Keep moving!" Jason pulled her along.

The pair didn't say much. Their chests heaved and panted and they cracked sticks and twigs as they hurried deeper into the forest.

"I need to rest." Tori finally collapsed. She scratched around the wound in her leg. "It itches something fierce."

Jason leaned over and placed his hands on his knees. "You think they'll chase us?"

"Maybe." Tori rubbed her thigh.

"Shit! We need to keep moving then."

"Just give me a few minutes."

Jason looked back the way they came. He moved from side to side trying to see through the trees, "I don't see 'em."

"That doesn't mean they aren't coming."

Jason wiped sweat from his brow and wiped it on his pants, "Yeah. You ready?"

Tori nodded. She got to her feet and tested her leg. The bleeding had stopped and it felt a little better. Jason took her arm.

"I think I can manage on my own."

"You probably have nerve damage. Let's not make it worse."

Tori resigned to let him help her and they continued to the west for several minutes. She panted and leaned against a mossy tree. Jason tore pieces of his shirt off to create bandages for her leg.

"It's feeling a lot better. It still aches, but the sharp pain is gone and it isn't bleeding at all."

"Let me see it." Jason kneeled down and moved her clothing to the side. To his surprise the dried blood had scabbed and only a small portion of the wound was open. "Holy cow!"

"What?"

"It looks like it's healing."

Tori pulled her pants to the side and looked down. "Well, it should be. Hopefully."

"No, I mean healing like super fast. Look at it."

"Still looks fucked up to me and hurts real bad."

Jason wiped sweat from his brow. "Tori, this is weird."

A large insect that looked like the combination of a praying mantis and wasp landed near him. He swatted at it with his hand to shoo it away.

"Well, this whole world is weird, Jason. All I care is that I can walk better."

Jason stood up and backed away from her. "Maybe you're infected?"

"Jason, if that were the case, I would have transformed by now. Other than today I have been in the compound working *inside* for the last week or better."

"It's just weird, Tori. That's all. I don't want to get infected."

"You think I do?" She stepped down from the log. "Give me the damn bandages."

Jason handed the strips from his shirt. "No need to get upset. I'm just saying if the roles were reversed I wouldn't want you to get sick."

Tori bandaged her leg, "Well, it's bad enough it might be true without you thinking so."

"I didn't mean anything by it." Jason waved his hand at another large bug buzzing by his ear.

"Jesus! That thing was huge!"

"Yeah, I just shooed one away a minute ago."

Tori stood up, "Yeah, but that one was the size of a small bird!"

"The one I swatted it was big, but I—"

"No, look." Tori pointed. "There are three or four of them up there about the size of birds."

Jason looked in awe and horror. "Let's get out of here." The insects took to the air. "Run!"

Tori limped away as fast as she could to keep up. The woods erupted in buzzing from tens of thousands of large insect wings. Green and yellow flashes swarmed to their right. Tori screamed and ran back left, but the swarm continued, clicking and diving at their heads and feet.

Tori shrieked and clung to Jason. He turned nervously, surrounded by circling flying giant mantis-like insects. Their whirling buzzing wings made a green and yellow tornadic blur around the pair. Jason futilely swatted at the cyclone if it got too close. The mantis-like bugs parted and a small woman, maybe five foot tall, walked toward them. She was naked and her milky skin created tantalizing shadows around her full breasts and collar bones. The cyclone settled in the forest around her, seemingly alive and moving with tens of thousands of bird sized insects.

"Who are you?" Jason shook nervously.

The woman stepped forward and looked Jason in the eyes. Jason placed his hand in front of Tori and stepped between them.

She cocked her head to the side and looked at Jason then at Tori. "You okay?"

Tori nodded. "Aren't you afraid of these bugs?"

The woman laughed, "No, child. You have not matured yet."

"Look, if these bugs are your pets, call them off. Some crazy zealots just killed all of our friends."

The woman looked to the east toward the compound. She pointed. "That way?"

Tori nodded distantly.

"That one there," the naked woman pointed at Jason. "I'll spare him since you seem attached. But when you mature, you will have no use for him."

Tori and Jason watched in disbelief as the woman strode to the east. Her swarm of bird sized mantis bugs took flight and followed her dipping and diving like a school of fish in the ocean.

"What the fuck was that?" Jason fell back against a tree.

"That was intense."

"Intense?" Jason groaned, grabbing his chest. "Intense? Three are a lot of things I would use to describe what we just saw and intense is not one of them."

"Do you think she controlled the bugs?"

"I... I don't know, Tori. Let's just get moving. The more distance we create from her and those zealots, the better."

Tori reluctantly started following Jason to the west. She was so enthralled with the woman and her swarm of insects she didn't even notice she wasn't limping.

"How many of the heathens are left?" The middle aged man in ragged bib over-alls thumbed a skinning knife. "'Cause I'm ready to get back as soon as possible."

"Hold your horses." Jacob shielded his eyes and looked across the grassy field to the west. "Say, you remember them two that got away?"

"Yup."

"Look there."

The middle aged man slipped his skinning knife in his belt sheath and shielded his eyes from the evening sun. He could see a small framed woman standing nude at the edge of the forest. "Well, I reckon that is one of 'em. I think they said her name was Tori."

"Where did her clothes go?"

"She naked?"

"Kinda' looks that away."

"Wanna' go drag her into them woods?"

Jacob smacked the other man in the shoulder. "Not a chance. We are righteous defenders of the Lord's commandments."

"Yeah, but she ain't holy or nuthin'. Barely even a woman."

Jacob put on his ball cap, "Well, let's go grab her"

The pair started walking across the grassy field. Jacob pointed and shook his finger at the woman. "Hey, you need to show some common decency!"

The woman paused, her light brown hair fluttered in the breeze. She looked up to the roof of the compound. A man aimed a sniper rifle at her. He hoisted a bulky radio to his mouth.

"This is watcher roof one. I got a naked female approaching the compound from the west. Looks like she has a bunch of rabbits or something following her under the tall grass. Can't tell. Something is moving around her. What do you want me to do with her?

The radio chirped back, "Is the ground crew going out to meet her?"

"Yep."

"Just cover them. A lone naked woman shouldn't be any problem."

The two men paused in the field. They kicked at the bird sized bugs moving through the grass under them. "What the hell?"

Jacob lifted his foot and stomped down, ignoring the woman as she neared. "Those some big ass, bugs."

The grass shook and trembled around them as the insects rushed passed.

"What did you want?" The woman folded her arms under her full breasts.

Jacob jumped. "Whoa, careful now. There is a swarm of bugs around here."

The woman didn't reply. She cast an arched eyebrow at the other man that was staring at her breasts.

"Um,..." Jacob stammered. "Look, you need to come with

us. Why are you naked? Are you hurt?"

"I'm not hurt and why I'm naked is none of your business."

Jacob frowned, "Now, don't sass me, you little bitch!"

The woman smiled, "I just needed to know your heart." She jabbed out her fingers and stabbed into Jacob's neck. In a quick motion, she jerked out his throat. The other man lifted his rifle, but the swarm was on him. They erupted from the grass—stinging and biting the men. They collapsed into the field under a swarming mass of insects.

"Holy shit!" The man on the roof took aim and fired. The insects erupted from the grass and formed a living wall in front of the woman. The rounds tore through their fragile insect bodies. Green and yellow gore erupted as the bullet slowed and fell harmlessly after passing through dozens of insects. The swarm reacted and tore out from the field and attacked the man on the roof. He screamed and tried to run from their buzz filled charge, but collapsed under their attack several feet from the ladder.

The woman set her eyes on the compound and the shouts from inside. A wicked smile crept across her tight lips as she stalked forward.

Gunfire erupted from the complex like lightning bugs in the dim evening as she strode to the front door. Hot lead struck thousands of her insects, but their numbers rendered the bullets harmless. Great gouts of green goo erupted from their chitinous bodies. They wounded bugs fell to the dry brown grass of the field, twitching before they died.

The Mantis Queen stepped through the side door of the compound. The cool air of the inside rushed over naked body. It had been a long time since she felt air conditioning. Her swarm of insects crowded into the tiny hallway. Shouts and screams erupted from the corridors as her swarm did its work. They swarmed each room and stung and mauled everyone inside. Room to room, they methodically slaughtered all that were within.

She knelt down next to two bodies. The barrels of their guns were still warm to the touch. Their eyes were wide with terror, barely able to blink from the mantis toxin surging through their veins. She smiled briefly at the tens of thousands of stings welts that covered their flesh. Small drops of yellowish green fluid dripped from the red welts. "You'll bring forth many new loves, my sweets," she stroked the paralyzed men's cheeks. "This compound will serve me well for my brood."

"And I will restore to you the years that the swarming locust has eaten, the crawling locust, and the consuming locust, and the cutting locust, my great army which I sent among you."

Joel 2:25

7
THE RAGE KING

Corey's huge muscled chest heaved with each breath as his heavy footfalls thudded on the hard Texas clay. He was getting close, he could feel it. The mighty rager wasn't sure what he was close to, his thoughts were always jumbled and confusing. But, something was calling him and it was getting nearer with every step. The behemoth rager stumbled and bumbled his way through the forest. His large muscled body snapped off branches and he trampled forest thistles and deadfalls as he thundered by. He popped over a ridge and froze in his tracks. He could see a large valley with a small creek running though the middle of it. The valley was covered in tall grass with an occasional small sapling standing like long hair from an unwanted mole. But what sent his heart into furious beats of excitement, were forty head of cattle, slowly grazing on the grass. Corey had not eaten in several days and he could feel his muscles beginning to atrophy.

Corey slowly climbed over the barbwire fence. The rusty wire bent down and snapped under his weight. His stomach growled so loud, he could feel it in his neck. Ducking low he advanced toward the fresh bloody beef he craved.

One of the cows looked directly at him. It swished its tail, ears forward in mild interest, before ducking its head back down to take another bite. Foot over foot, he crouched low in the tall grass like a clumsy lion stalking an unconcerned bison. Closer he drew. When he was thirty feet away, he paused. This was his shot.

Erupting from the tall grass, Corey's muscled body flexed, driving him forward. His bare feet slipped on the weeds and he stumbled forward. With a flailing attempt, he reached out for the cow, his heavy body striking the animal under the haunches. The cow kicked lightly and sprung from his grasp. His meaty fingers slid down the short furred bovine with nothing to hold on to. Striking the ground, Corey's other hand latched on to the bottom of the animal's rear leg. It kicked back as it ran, hitting Corey in the face and shoulder a few times. He tried to maintain his one hand hold while being drug and jerked down the dirt cow path in the middle of the tall grass. But before long, the cow wrenched itself free. The herd mooed loudly in protest as the cow trotted off, further down the valley, its tail twitching back and forth in angry frustration.

Corey weakly sat up and stared at the hill he had come from. The cows mooed and continued away from him while his dull witted mind tried to formulate some sort of new tactic. The sound of thundering hoof beats behind him roused him from his difficult thoughts. Turning from the seated position, Corey caught the glimpse of two long curled horns of a bull just as it struck him in the face and shoulders. He closed his eyes and flash of bright lights erupted behind his eyelids. His heavy body was tossed effortlessly into the air. He flailed out before striking the hard earth. He was slightly confused and dizzy. He managed to get to all fours before being struck a second time. The bull's long horn ripped through his side. Pain flooded into Corey's mind. Rage. The rage came. The rager snarled, turning into the impalement and wrapping his arm around the bull's head, he got to his feet and twisted his upper body. The horn that was impaled into his side snapped like a small stick under then rager's power. His thick tree trunk legs flexed and the monster that was once a man, twisted the bull's head. The animal lost its footing and was flipped to its side. Snarling Corey rained down a tremendous blow to the beast's neck, but to his surprise, the bull was covered in matted fur revealing rough and scaly yellow skin. The beast continued to roll, and pulled Corey over the top of him, slinging him through the air to the other side. Corey landed hard on his shoulder and slid lifelessly through the grass. He recovered quickly and used the momentum to get to his feet at the same time he ripped the long horn from his body. The wound immediately began to heal and he held the long broken horn like a gladiator's sword about to face off against a lion in the arena.

The bull tossed its head for balance and regained its footing. It's broken horn bled from its skull briefly before beginning to reform before Corey's eyes. The animal's fur patched yellow hide covered massive rippling muscles more akin to a Belgian Blue than a typical pasture guardian. The beast snorted and lowered its head. It pawed at the ground, snorting a violent and guttural snort. It all clicked in his mind. The bull was infected. It was a rager.

Corey frowned with hatred and resolve and started toward the monster. He hoisted the horn over his head as he charged to plunge it into the body of the beast he faced.

The bull's shoulder lurched and its powerful back legs flexed, kicking up great clods of dirt as it charged. The two met in a thunderous clap of meat. Their two powerful bodies colliding. Corey felt his ribs shatter and his shoulder snapped and the bone stabbed through his flesh. He brought the horn down with his other hand, striking the monstrous bull in the snout. Blood, spit, and snot erupted from the animal's head, its eyes rolled back, and the monster fell to the earth unconscious.

Corey groaned and snarled in pain, shoving his bone back into his flesh the best he could before it would heal. He didn't bother making sure it would heal exactly right, his limited intelligence wasn't even worried about such things.

He stalked over to the bull, grimacing with each mighty breath that forced his shattered ribs to stab into his soft organs. His left shoulder wasn't healed enough for him to lift and it hung loosely at his side. Bright red blood streamed from his wound and dripped from his fingers, covering the light brown grass like a splatter of paint.

He raised the horn over his head to smash the head of his enemy when the bull's eyes opened. Corey stared into the monster's eyes and he felt a connection. The bull got to his feet and shook his head, but quickly regained the gaze into Corey's eyes.

Corey wasn't sure what the animal said, but he patted it on the neck. He wasn't angry anymore. He wasn't sure why, but he liked the bull now. Maybe it was the worthy battle they just shared. It was like he could hear what the bull was saying to him, but the animal did not speak. It was more of emotion than anything. But, what he did gather, was that there was a farm house up the hill a ways and lots of food for his kind there.

Corey smiled and started walking to the farm house. The bull walked next to him, both no longer concerned with the herd of cows that had taken refuge in a small grove of trees up the far hill away from the farm house.

Corey hopped the fence and started toward the house. It was fairly small as houses went. There were several large barns, but they were the old style with wooden plank sides and silver tin roofs. He turned to see the bull had paused at the fence. It was weird. Corey could hear the animal speaking to him in thoughts even if he was not making eye contact.

Corey walked back and grabbed the wooden fence post. Even in his weakened state, he was able to wrench it from the ground. He felt the bones in shoulder that didn't heal properly, snap under the force of his muscle. He growled in pain and tossed the wooden fence post with the barbed wire to the side. The bull sniffed the ground briefly before stepping though. The pair made their way to the farm house. He could see two silver grain bins near a tractor next to the barn. He walked over to the tractor. He grabbed the front tie rod of the tractor and ripped it loose. He smashed it into the side of the grain bin, over and over again until a small hole had formed. He continued to smash until the tie rod snapped. A small bit of corn started to leak out and spill onto the ground. Corey turned to grab another tie rod when he noticed six other ragers coming from the farm. Two were normal height like he was, but the other four, they were almost nine feet tall. Three were male and one was female. Their naked bodies were lean from malnutrition. They all stared into his eyes and he could hear their emotions, just like the bull's. Corey readied himself to fight, but they just stood there confused.

Corey cautiously ripped loose the other tie rod and paused to see if they would attack, but they just stood silently and motionless, like a statue. He turned and smashed the tie rod into the small hole in the grain bin before glancing back to see if they were charging. When he was satisfied they were not going to move, he hammered the tie rod over and over into the small hole of the grain bin until it was large enough that a steady stream of corn poured out from it and made a large pile on the ground. Corey and the bull crunched their fill of corn. He could almost instantly feel his full strength returning. He looked at the others and urged them to come forward. They all came forward, calmly and politely. He had never seen others like him. The ferals were uncontrollable and always had to be fought. But, these types were different.

Corey snatched up his horn and patted the bull on the side. The name "Apis" came to his mind. He smiled. Corey knew he could not speak, but the bull seemed to hear his thought and enjoy it.

The pull came again. It was getting close. Corey felt the urgency. He started jogging down the farm lane toward the road. Apis, and the six ragers trotted behind. They ran for most of the day, pausing on a dirt ridge covered with forest trees overlooking a highway. Corey could feel the pull coming from down the road, but it was getting closer. They would wait. Soon the time to claim this unknown desire would be upon him.

"How is she holding up?" Chris glanced back over his shoulder.

"Looks to be her happy self," Sarah slid a lock of her hair behind her ear. "How far are we from Springfield?"

Sammy silently stared off into the west. The setting sun painted a myriad of colors across the evening sky.

"We haven't hit Branson yet. Check the map and see if we drive through it."

Artez fumbled around in the glove box and opened an atlas map book. "It's almost dark, mind flipping on the light?"

Chris clicked on the dome light and Artez leaned over. "Yeah, looks like we run right through the east side of Branson."

Chris frowned, "Any bypass routes?"

"Doesn't look like it. We can take a major detour and head up this 265, but man that's a long way around."

"How much of the city will we go through?"

"Enough that if they have set up barricades or want to trap us, they'll be able to do it pretty easily."

"Fuck." Chris grabbed his radio. "Scout-1 to Warthog."

"Warthog, go ahead."

"Yeah, looks like we're coming up on Branson. No safe way through it by looking at the map. I want to pull off and set camp. We can send a scout unit up the road and see if the city has fortified the interstate."

"Sounds good."

Chris pulled Scout-1 to the side of the road. He got out of the car and walked back to the others. Everyone was getting out of the vehicles and grouping up.

"Do you think this is wise?" Chad asked. "My daughter isn't still pretty banged up."

Chris nodded, "We can monitor her well and we are only about ten miles out. The ZRVs can get there and back pretty quick and also remain in radio contact."

"Fair enough," Chad turned and went back to his daughter.

"The real question," Chris began again, "Is who's going to go?"

George raised his hand. His unkempt curly brown hair waved in the evening breeze. "I'll go. Levi says he's in, too."

Tibbs looked at Terry as they leaned against the Warthog's bumper, "I'll go."

Terry raised his hand and nodded, "I'm in."

Chris smiled, "Okay, great. Make sure you're armored up. Don't engage anyone, just scout and come back and report."

"What vehicle do you want us to take?"

"Take the Vipers. They won't use as much gas and ATVs will be much more quiet."

Brian smiled, "Damn. Had I know we were breaking them out I would have volunteered. Love driving them."

Everyone had a hearty laugh.

THE APOCALYPSE OF ENOCH

April sat under a shade tree in the hot Texas sun. She wiped sweat from her brow and gently brushed her hair with an old plastic brush she found in an abandoned trailer. Vorto scooted around on the hot asphalt road in front of her chasing grasshoppers and other beetles. He would giggle with delight when he caught one before popping it into his mouth and crunching it under his large teeth.

"You're one creepy little dude," April shook her head.

Vorto stopped what he was doing and looked at April when she spoke. The little monster loved hearing her voice.

April smiled and kept brushing. She sipped on a hot soda and her mind wandered back to her broadcasting days. She thought about what led her to this point and she wondered how her family in Arkansas faired.

Vorto roused her from her doldrums. His small boney gray hand pulled on her wrist.

"What do you want, Vorto? I'm trying to relax."

Vorto kept pulling and smiled at her with his soft big eyes.

April sighed, sliding the brush in her pocket. She stood and let Vorto lead her out from under the cool shade and across the hot sun baked Texas clay. "Vorto, I'm not really interested in bugs."

The small creature smiled and made some sort of cooing sound and kept leading her. His other hand scooted him awkwardly across the dirt until he stopped and pointed between two large rocks in a creek bed.

"You wanted to show me rocks?"

Vorto growled and pointed again.

"Vorto, I don't care." April wrenched her hand free and started back to her tree when she heard a rattle snake rattle. She froze in her tracks. "Vorto, be careful! There's a rattle snake!"

Vorto ignored her and scooted to the edge of the creekbed. The small front wheels of his lawn mower bottom crunched small clods over the side.

April glanced around and realized the sound was coming from the creek. She moved next to Vorto. "Careful, I think the snake is..." her eyes caught a wooden handle sticking out of the sand between the two rocks. It sounded like the rattle was coming from the handle. She sat down on her butt and scooted over the side and down into the creekbed. Small bits of dirt fell down behind her. She slid to the bottom and made her way over to the two rocks. She could clearly see the handle and the sound was louder than ever.

Take it. The voice in her head sounded. It had been several days since she had heard it.

She leaned down and gently pulled on the handle. It broke loose from the dry sand. It was a long wooden shaft on the end that was buried under the sand was a turtle shell lashed together with leather that was wrapped around the end of the stick.

"Did you see this?"

Vorto clicked and hummed excitedly. He clasped his hands under his chin and smiled. His large eyes beamed with excitement.

April moved to the edge of the dry creek bed. Setting the rattle on the ledge, she grunted, hoisting herself up.

Vorto gazed down at the rattle in wide wonderment. His lips pursed in excitement, "OoooooOOOoooooo."

April got to her feet and dusted the dry Texas clay from her butt. She picked up the rattle and examined it further.

This is of your people. It will serve you, the voice sounded. April had become accustomed to the voice. It wasn't male or female, she couldn't quite put a gender on it. It was soothing and comforting. She couldn't help but trust its guidance.

Vorto reached out with his index finger and touched the bottom tip of the handle. "oooOOOoooo."

"What do you think it is?" April smiled at Vorto.

He just looked up in wonderment. He smiled back and blinked at her. "Natcha."

April smiled, "Vorto. You spoke."

He nodded, "Natcha."

"So, what is a Natcha."

Vorto pointed at the turtle shell rattle and then back April. "Natcha."

April laughed, "Just when I thought you were actually saying something."

THE APOCALYPSE OF ENOCH

"*Every man is brutish in his knowledge: every founder is confounded by the graven image: for his molten image is falsehood, and there is no breath in them. They are vanity, and the work of errors: in the time of their visitation they shall perish.*"

Jeremiah 10:14-15

8
ORBS

The soft hum of the ZRVs off road tires echoed off of the asphalt. The cool night wind made Tibbs's eyes water and stream thinly down his cheeks. The nearby mountainous hills of the Ozarks over looked the four as they neared Branson. George brought his ZRV to a slow and then pulled to the shoulder. The other's followed.

"So..." Tibbs tuned his ignition off and stretched his back.

"Right up this hill is Branson."

Terry rubbed his side. It still ached from the gunshot wound he suffered months ago. "So, do we drive up? Walk up?"

"I vote we drive up." Tibbs patted his belly. "I been losing my gut since the world fell apart and that was part of my charm."

Levi got on the radio, "Viper-2 to Scout-1."

"Scout-1," the radio chirped.

Levi flinched and turned the radio down, "Chris, Branson is about a half mile from us, at the top of the hill. The ZRVs are pretty quiet, but the tires are loud as shit on the asphalt. Should we go the rest of the way on foot?"

"Um, how big is the hill?"

"Well, I mean, it's typical for this area."

George scanned the horizon, "What I wouldn't do for a spotter and a rifle."

"Do what George wants to do," the radio chirped. "Just remember Sammy and the little girl don't have forever."

"10-4."

"Well?" Tibbs's raspy voice broke the silence.

"Up to George."

George bit his lip, "Look guys. This is what we have. We can make great time on the ZRVs. We can get in and get out. Down side, if they want to control the interstate, they likely will hear us and beef up."

"What if we go in on foot?" Terry asked.

"If we go in on foot and shit hits the fan, we might not be able to get back to the ZRVs."

Tibbs laid back on the seat and looked up at the brilliant twinkling starry night, "I'm good for wasting the night away watching the stars. I don't get to see much of them in Cali."

"Okay, let's just ride and see what is going on. We can always turn around. I doubt they'll want to chase us. And, if they don't want us to go through, we just head back and circle around." Terry suggested.

George nodded, "Sounds good. Let's do it."

"The star watching, or Terry's bad idea."

They group got on their ATVs and started them up.

"Well, I guess that answers that," Tibbs chuckled.

The whimpering moans of her captives echoed in the large garage of the ZOD complex. Twenty one, she counted. Their bodies were cocooned in a gelatinous goo that held them all against the walls. They would replenish her swarms in a few days. If they lived for the rest of the week, she could double, maybe triple her swarm.

"What are you?" Dean's lower lip quivered weakly.

The woman slinked forward. Her naked body seemed nearly perfect in the pale light of the garage. She reached up and grabbed him by the chin, "Before the Rapture, my name was Meegan. But, I have been empowered by God to scour the earth and sweep clean the plague of man."

Dean coughed up blood. His weak body hung loosely by

a sticky green gel that attached him to the wall. "Have mercy. I'm just a simple talent scout from Britain," he mumbled with his thick English accent.

"Mercy?" Meegan laughed. "Do you not know who I am? I am the rider on a pale horse. I am death incarnate. I have been empowered to kill the wickedness of man with plague and pestilence."

"What have you done to us?" A zealot in white moaned. "You don't serve the one true God."

"I serve the one true God. The alpha and the omega. The first and the last. And your wicked flesh will serve me before it perishes back to the earth from which it was formed."

The zealot spit on the floor, "You work the will of Satan."

Meegan laughed. Her swarm of mantis wasps writhed and clicked on the ceiling, making it sway and roll like the ocean. "The Morning Star is not here. But, the old gods will come. We horseman are to scour the land before his coming. To punish the sons and daughters of man for their wickedness."

"I'm not wicked. I'm just a talent agent," Dean pleaded.

Meegan lifted his chin and kissed his forehead, "My sweet fool, you are wicked. You very nature is wickedness. But, fear not. Your misery will last a short while and then it will end."

Screams erupted in the garage. The men and women struggled against their bonds, but they could not break free. The eggs injected into their flesh from the stings began to hatch. The larvae burrowed into their skin.

Meegan closed her eyes and moved her hands in a melodic dance to their screams. She smiled knowing her swarm would be growing soon.

Tori and Jason made their way through the night. Her leg had pretty much healed all the way and she was able to outpace Jason. She was frustrated at how slow he moved. He gasped and wheezed, holding his hands to his chest. "My God, Tori. Slow down."

She turned and glared at him, "Slow down? Are you insane?"

"I can't keep up. I'm tired and my feet are numb. I need to rest."

Tori rolled her eyes, she was the one that was shot in the leg. "You cry like a little girl."

"Tori, I'm sorry. How are you even running?"

She paused for a moment and looked down at her blood soaked pant leg. The fresh gunshot wound didn't even ache. She bit her lip and stuck her finger inside. "It must have not been that bad. I think it's scabbed up pretty good."

Jason leaned against a tree and vomited. "I need to rest for the night. I don't know where you're going in such a hurry, but surely we are safe from the crazy ass bug lady."

Tori pointed ahead, "As soon as we clear that chain link fence, there is a building we can rest in."

Jason frowned and strained his eyes through the darkness, "How can you see that?"

Tori shrugged, "It ain't that dark. Come on."

Jason groaned and doggedly staggered after her.

Tori reached the fence. She stuck her toes into the chain links and grabbed the top bar. With a quick hop, she effortlessly cleared it.

Jason leaned on the outside of the fence, "Just go. I'll catch up in a minute."

Tori shook her head, "I'm going to check the building for supplies. Looks like a veterinary office or something."

"Just be careful." Jason grabbed his chest and sat down on the ground. He laid his head back against the cool metal.

Tori neared the building. It was fairly large. Dark green moss had grown up the side of the red brick. She moved to the front. There was single glass door that had the words "Cerberus, do not enter" spray painted in red. The red had run down the glass like small trails of blood.

She checked the handle, and the door was locked. Its metal frame rattled against the deadbolt.

Go inside. The voice in her head commanded. Tori pinched the bridge of her nose. She was losing it. She pulled a little harder on the door, and to her surprise, the glass shattered and the frame bent, pulling the dead bolt out of the wall. Her thoughts on the weak door were interrupted by the barks and guttural growls coming from inside the building.

Tori stepped inside the hallway. Her shoes crunched the broken glass. There was a small waiting room with plastic chairs. An end table was covered in magazines. A fogged window was closed and there was a single wooden door to the back that was cracked open. Slowly, but deliberately, she moved down the hall. Outstretching her hand, she lightly pushed the door open. The hinges creaked, revealing several dozen kennels. Dogs barked and snapped at their cages in a ferocious feral display. Their fur was spotty at best and their skin was crusted and overgrown. Tori moved around the back and rummaged through cabinets. She found large garbage cans full of dog food. The dogs seemed to calm themselves. Despite being infected, they were thin and seemed to be wasting away. Tori couldn't bring herself to ignore them. She scooped the dog food and started filling their food bowls. The animals wagged their tail and crunched the food in merriment.

"Tori?" Jason poked his head into the room. "You okay?"

Tori turned and looked at him. He seemed blind in the low lit room. "Yeah, I just couldn't leave them like this."

Jason backed up in fear. He held the aluminum bar from the front door in his hand. "T-Tori. What's wrong with your eyes?"

Tori frowned. "Nothing is wrong with my eyes."

"They're glowing."

"Don't be silly." She dumped another scoop into the dog's kennels.

"No, really." Jason backed slowly out of the room. "They're glowing bright white color."

"That's nonsense, Jason."

"Find a mirror, Tori. I'm not lying."

Tori groaned, "Whatever, we need food and supplies. There isn't much here."

Jason stood in the door way, "I'm gonna go, Tori."

"Okay, I'll be out in a minute."

Jason backed away from the doorway and started out of the front door. The impending terror crept behind him, like a child rushing to his bed to hide under the covers. He couldn't resist the urge to break out into a run. Dashing from the front door he ran out into the night.

Tori went to the kennels one by one. The dogs growled and snarled until she made eye contact with them. They seemed to calm when she did. She could tell they were frustrated at being locked up. She wasn't sure how she knew, but it was like their feelings were speaking to her without uttering a sound. She was surprised at herself when she opened the kennel door, and more surprised that the infected dog did not attack her. It's massively powerful muscles rippled under its crusted skin. One by one she uncrated the rager dogs, and one by one, they all climbed from their kennels and took in file behind her. She wasn't sure what kind of dogs they were. She guessed pit bull by their heart shaped heads and muscled frames. Some of the dogs had cut ears and some didn't, but they all followed her without question.

Your transformation is complete, the voice in her head echoed, *Now go forth, and purge this land of the wicked. You are a Nephilim of Conquest. The beasts of the earth will serve you.*

Tori stepped from the shelter into the cool night air. "Jason?" She called out, but he was nowhere to be found. The dogs fanned out behind her in a powerful pack of teeth and death. She was disappointed that Jason had left, but it was likely for the best. His weak heart would only get in her way.

"Check the power," Sargent Fipps frowned. He twisted the pliers on the wire and crimped it down.

"Okay, it's locked in. Tell me when to fire her up." John Paul dusted his hands off.

Sargent Fipps tightened the bolt down and secured the cable, "Okay, here we go." He flipped the switch and the hydraulic battle suit roared to life. It stood up, maybe eight feet in full height. One arm had a jack hammer and the other arm had a large claw. It was made out of crudely welded quarter inch steel and the interior of the legs had folding pegs that allowed a pilot to climb in. A roll cage cockpit protected with steel plating had a plethora of levers and handles inside.

"Woo hoo!" Sargent Fipps cheered, "One more skeleton for the ORBS squad!"

John Paul gave the sergeant a high five. "That's it, though. We have scoured the entire city for more Segways—none to be found. I'm not sure what else has the tilt sensors, so for now, you better take care of the four we have."

Sargent Fipps smiled, "Well, four is a rocking amount. We will be able to do some monster damage to those fucking ragers."

John flipped off the power source. "I'll get it set up and loaded up. Scouts report that a large group of ragers was gathering south of here."

"I'm hitting the rack, JP. Goodnight." Sargent Fipps watched John leave the workshop. He stared at the battle suit in the dimly lit garage. He had seem some pretty epic combat fighting these disgusting monsters. They had been careful not to deploy against more than a dozen—and even then their battle suits had been severally damaged and they lost one pilot.

Tibbs and the others broke the crest of the hill. The interstate was cut into the deep Ozark bedrock around them. A spider web of exits and onramps covered the area. An overhead traffic light lit the interstate and many of the houses to the west had power.

The group slowed their ZRVs.

"Look at that," Terry pointed. "I'd kill for a hot shower."

"No need to worry about making contact, looks like we have a crew coming to see us."

Tibbs glanced nervously behind them, "Might be time to bail back down the road."

"Nope!" Levi pointed at the jeep, "Look on the side. It's a ZERV."

THE APOCALYPSE OF ENOCH

George laughed, "How many damn ZOD members are there? I'd never heard of the group before shit hit the fan. Now, it seems they're the only ones prepped for surviving."

"There were several zombie fighting groups across the US. Even another one in Saint Louis, but they weren't equipped to deal with what went down like ZOD was." Levi rubbed his beard, "It doesn't surprise me at all that ZOD emerged in all this mess."

"Okay, well let's be ready just in case they're hostile. Granted, they might have been in the same nerd group before the collapse, but that doesn't mean they're going to be friendly."

The jeep approached and rolled to a stop. It had a lot of damage on the outside, including holes from gun fire. The driver turned the vehicle to the side, perpendicular to the group. He wore a red beret and a black tactical uniform consistent with members of ZOD. "I'm going to guess you aren't federation?"

George shook his head, "Not sure who the federation is, but we're ZOD members from Texas. We have an infected member we're trying to get to the medical unit in Springfield. We think she has a mutated strain that could offer a cure."

The man stepped out of the jeep. He was a large man, maybe six foot three and just over three hundred pounds, and had short blond hair. His clothes fit him loosely. "The name is Naylor. Rick Naylor. I'm with the Ozark chapter. We're a little thin on members. Been fighting the Ozark Christian Federation and a fuckton of ragers."

"Why would a Christian Federation be shooting at you?"

Rick laughed, "Well, they aren't your normal Christians. Seems all the real ones I knew turned into monsters. These are the over top fire and brimstone types. Think Westboro without laws and with lots of fucking guns."

"Sounds terrible."

"The increase amount of ragers have them thinned out pretty good. But, they are gaining momentum. Springfield reports they have been attacked several times this week."

George rubbed his chin, "Our convoy is pretty well armed. We aren't looking for a fight, but we have several vehicles and about fifteen soldiers."

"Well, we can spare a vehicle or two, once you get here. Ya' know, help you make it all the way up. I'd be more worried about the ragers than the federation."

Terry turned on his ATV, "We don't have a lot of time. We'll be rolling through soon. But, I thought ragers pretty much ran by themselves?"

"They used to," Rick climbed back in his jeep. "But here lately they've been collecting and hanging out in certain areas. Not fighting themselves much. Makes me wonder if they're trying to recall their human side and build communities, or if there's something more sinister going on."

"Thanks for the heads up," George turned on his ATV. "We'll be back with our crew in about thirty minutes or so."

"If you think you have a cure, it might be better to send some ORBS with you."

"ORBS?"

Rick nodded, "Outbreak Response Battle Suits. We got the plans sent to us from Nevada unit via satellite."

"So, there are people in Nevada?" Tibbs's eyes lit up. "That means California might be okay?"

"Maybe," Rick ran his hands through his hair. "But, with Yellowstone erupting and all that, anything much west a' Kansas is nothun' but scorched earth."

"Wait, Yellowstone erupted?" Levi was in disbelief.

"Yup."

"Like a volcano erupted?"

"I done said yup. The whole damn park was a giant super volcano. Didn't you notice how it got cold for that month? The soot and ash blocked out the sun."

"What's this scorched earth?" Tibbs pinched his nose. Getting home was going to be even harder.

"Yup. Covered in ash and soot and shit." Rick nodded, "We even got a chapter in Iowa—some place called Broken Bow—done said there is some Indian witch doctors summoning the dead right out the ground."

"How long will it take for the ORBS to get here?" George looked down at his watch. He wasn't going to let this turn into some sort of superstitious discussion and waste more time.

"Let me call the sarge." Rick picked up the radio.
"What do you think?" Tibbs glanced around nervously.
"Not sure, but it sounds like it could be help. What could it hurt to wait?"

Rick hung the radio up on the dash. "After he stopped cursing for being woken up, he said he would be up with two suits. "

"Well, I guess we wait just a little bit."

Corey sat on the ridge and looked below. The setting sun cast oranges and violets across the horizon. He could see several vehicles — all black. They had some odd symbol on the side. He didn't read, or even comprehend the idea of reading. But, he knew his journey had brought him to this moment. What he was supposed to do was inside that front car. It was his master. His savior. His friend, and she was trapped. He watched the men get on the smaller vehicles and drive off to the north. But, he could hear her. She wasn't ready for him yet. Corey stroked the neck of Apis. The golden patchy fur covered bull seemed to understand his intent. It was time.

"And there we saw the Nephilim, and we seemed to ourselves like grasshoppers, and so we seemed to them."

Numbers 13:33

9
DESOLATION

Meegan rifled through a closet in the decimated ZOD compound. Piles of clothes and equipment littered the small storage room. She preferred to be nude, and rely on her swarms to do her bidding, but battling the zealots had taught her that she needed to be as efficient at killing as her insects were. Clothing was so restrictive, but it was going to be necessary.

"What an annoying day," She examined a leather shoulder holster and tossed it into a pile of old ZOD uniforms and equipment. She mulled over the gear as best she could before opting for a dingy blood stained tight fitting V-neck shirt that had 'Brolo Nation' written across the front of it. She liked that the second 'o' in Brolo looked kind of like an anarchy sign. Opting for a pair of black combat boots with the red ZOD logo on the outside of them and some cut off black tactical pants, turned daisy dukes, she strapped on her twin desert eagle shoulder holsters. The large pistols looked ridiculous on her small thin frame, but she knew she was more than strong enough to handle the weapons and the high grain rounds would tear apart the flesh of whatever they hit.

Meegan gave herself a once over in the mirror, before putting her light brown hair into a pony tail and slipping on a black ZOD officer's cap. She ducked in the mirror, low enough to see under the cracked bullet hole in the corner. Everything looked in order, but she felt her pistols could use some color. 'Later,' she thought.

The Mantis Queen strolled through the halls of the compound toward the garage. It had been made fairly battle ready. Most of the area outside the windows had been cleared for line of site and boarded or barred. Rooms had been quartered off depending on their use and it looks like they even had set up a fair sized medical bay. She stepped over the body of a large man. His shirt was torn open revealing an almost healed wound to his shoulder and ribs amid the gapping bloody injuries that caused his death. She smiled, thinking that he cheated death once before he finally got what he deserved.

Meegan popped to attention. She could feel the connection forming of tens of thousands of new mantises. She ran back through the desolated compound. Bursting into the garage, a wry smile crept on her face. Her once hundred thousand swarm was easily in the millions. They gathered on the ceiling, their wings beating and humming in a rhythmic chant while their bright green chitinous bodies writhed to and fro like ocean waves crashing against a shore.

She looked to her captured slaves, but was surprised to find only bloody chains and ropes where they had been. Pieces of gore, flesh, and entrails hung loosely from the confines that once held the bodies aloft. Only the zealot remained. She walked toward him, jerking his head upright by his sweaty hair. "What happened to my other incubators?"

He looked up, his eyes were heavy and from exhaustion and fear. "Your abomination ate their flesh."

"Abomination?" Meegan glanced around the garage. She could see a hulking shadow huddled under one of the work benches. She walked toward it and kneeled, cocking her head sideways to look at it. The beast was mostly human shaped. It had no skin, save for greenish pink patches between its dark green and black jagged chitinous shell that resembled fourteenth century armor more than it did an insect. Its hands were single hooked claws and its forearms bore down hundreds of spikes curved backward like a mantis. The monsters head was more mantis than human, with dozens of spikes splayed back from its head. Three pairs of long wasp shaped wings covered its back, reminding Meegan more of biblical descriptions of top tier angels than of her insects. "Oh, you're new." She said with a smile.

She reached out and stroked the monster's head. It turned to her quickly with its bright green human eyes. The beast quivered and shook, clicking odd insect like noises at her.

"Don't worry, my sweet. I'm not sure how you formed, but we must begin gathering more and more damned souls to make you some brothers and sisters. But, in the mean time, start with that zealot."

The anthropomorphic beasts looked at the man in chains and then back to Meegan. It shook its head from side to side. Meegan was frustrated that she could not understand the monster's thoughts like she could her swarm. She could feel a connection, but it was not one like she was accustomed to. Angered, she grabbed a wrench from the work table and stormed over to the zealot. "What sorcery has prevented my swarm from feeding on you?"

"I am with God." The man said weakly.

Meegan narrowed her eyes, "You are nothing. You are a plague to be eradicated. You are not with God."

"I am with him now," the man mumbled, "He is next to me."

Meegan grabbed his chin in her hands. She squeezed tightly until should could feel the bones in his jaw beginning to flex before she crushed it.

Stop. You may not harm this man! The voice echoed in her head. *I will mark all of those you may not kill with a symbol. You are the Nephilim of Death. Go forth, and spread my influence.*

Meegan snarled, "I may not be able to harm you overtly, but I know the true wickedness in your heart. You wouldn't be here, if not. So, enjoy your torment in these chains in this hot garage. I give you two days tops, before you die.

The man lowered his head. His sweaty hair tumbled down and hung before his face.

Meegan hit the button to the garage door and raised it. Her swarm writhed and dived anxiously until it shot out from under the garage into the open air. *Corpus Christi,* she thought. *I think that would make a great Bug Town.*

Sammy sat up from the back seat. Her sweaty long blonde hair stuck to her face. Her eyes and perspiration glowed a bright red in the darkness. She smiled devilishly. "You might want to run from me."

Sara frowned, "Why's that Sammy? Are you feeling okay?"

Chris opened the driver's side door and leaned in, "Sarah, the guys think they've got some coffee going."

"Oh man, that'd be sweet. Maybe get some for Sammy, too?"

"Too late." Sammy said with a smile. "You're too late."

April stared at the odd shaped stick with the turtle shell on the end. Vorto wouldn't take his eyes from it and often reached out to touch it, but shrieked and pulled his hand back every time like a child touching a hot stove. *A little bit further,* the voice in her head drove her forward. *Your third great grandmother escaped a slave plantation in Arkansas in 1860. She was taken in by a Seminole Indian family. They moved west after the devastating loss in the third great war with the whites. They settled here.*

"Who are you?" April asked. "You can't be some delusion. At least, I don't think that anymore."

Who I am, means nothing. Just know that I am.

"How are you communicating with me?"

It matters little how, but rather, focus on the truth that I am.

April rubbed her head. She stopped walking and leaned against the bumper of an abandoned car. "Okay, so you have guided me to this stick, told me some of what I already know about my heritage, and told me to come in this direction. Where am I going?"

You are here. I see that which is hidden. I know your heart. You will serve me.

THE APOCALYPSE OF ENOCH

April shook her head back and got her sweaty hair out of her face, "I'm a hot mess. I got no business doing anything right now other than finding a bath."

There will be time for that. But, now. Now is the time to retake the lands of your ancestors. Purge it of the unclean and the ungodly whom committed genocide against your people. Touch the earth with your scepter and watch your people rise.

April looked at the weird turtle shell headed stick. She bit her lip and frowned, reluctant to do what seemed like an order from a mental illness. But, she couldn't deny that it felt real. April cocked her head to the side and touched the dry parched ground with the end of the scepter. The wind picked up and blew dust around her. She could hear the songs of millions of Native Americans singing out from the earth in unison. Vorto giggled and looked around with wide eyes, ignoring the stinging dust in his eyes.

The earth cracked and yellowed bony fingers clawed their way up from the dirt. White bleached skulls with dark empty sockets that emitted a pale gray glow crested from the ground. April knew she should be terrified. She knew that there was no way this could be real. She knew she should run, scream, cower, but she did not of those. Instead, she marveled at what she created. There was a beauty and harmony in these walking bones. They were smooth, innocent, devoid of lusts of the flesh. April stood in awe for several minutes until over a hundred of these skeletons stood before her. Some hunched over, some missing limbs, but she could feel a powerful love and respect coming from each one. Their souls were never allowed to flee from their bones into eternal rest. But now, now they could begin to fulfill that purpose. She understood that every corpse that fell in battle to retake her homeland, would finally have its soul released. Florida would be hers once again, the way it should have been, the way her creator had decreed it always was going to be.

"Too late?" Chris wiped sweat from his bald head. The hum of the four wheel tires took his attention to the crest of the hill. Tibbs and the others broke the horizon and behind them was an odd looking Ford with huge tractor counter weights on the front bumper.

Sarah opened her door, "What are they hauling in the back of that truck?"

"Looks like some sort of heavy equipment."

"Incoming!" Artez raised his rifle to his shoulder and fired.

Chris looked over the top of his car in horror. A large group of ragers rushed down the hill next to the road. Dust and dirt kicked up from the tall brown grass surrounding them in an obscured cloud that floated in the hot dark night time air. He raised his rifle and fired. Hot lead tore into the massive hulking bodies.

Hitting the ditch, Corey stumbled. He tucked his head and somersaulted before regaining his feet at the edge of the road. Hot lead tore into his chest and thigh. He lowered his shoulder and smashed into the side of the truck. The flat black door caved in under his weight. He reached up and grabbed the stunned person on the other side. He squeezed his powerful grip on the man's shoulder. Bones snapped and the man screamed in pain. Corey's massive muscles flexed as he struggled to pull the man from the car. The frail body went limp and become stuck in the window. Enraged, Corey placed his foot up on the fender and pulled a second time. The body tore in half. Corey tossed the upper torso into the road and ripped the door off. He forced his over-sized body into the cab, but could not find what he was searching for. His pale yellow eyes watched the driver run into the woods before being trampled and mauled by Apis.

"Stay down, honey." Chad turned his gaze from Katie back to the chaos in front of him. Even being a top three gun shooter, he was unable to fell one of the beasts in the dim Missouri night.

Katie could hear the chaotic scene and the screams of dying men outside their vehicle. She wanted to help. She knew that even in her injured state, she could outshoot the other men.

Sammy watched the scene unfold. When her eyes met Corey's, she knew he was the one that she had been calling. She effortlessly snapped her handcuffs and opened the door. She moved behind Sarah and intertwined her hand in the back of Sarah's hair.

"Sammy?!" Sarah shrieked in surprise and struggled against Sammy's unnaturally strong grasp. "How did you?"

Sammy slammed Sarah's head down into the right quarter panel of Scout-1. Her skull collapsed under the force of the blow. Blood and bone dripped down the side of the shiny black car. Sammy smiled and turned her bright glowing red eyes toward Shane. There was a price to pay for being a leader of men.

"Oh fuck, oh fuck, oh fuck!" Tibbs ducked behind his four wheeler. "This pistol is fucking worthless. We might as well be shooting bears!"

Terry fired his pistols toward the mass of giant hulking ragers. One turned, snarled, and charged them. George, Levi, Terry, and Tibbs opened fire. The beast brought two heavy fists down onto Terry, smashing him under the force of the blow. Two tires of the four wheeler tore from the rims and the vehicle bent and twisted under the incredible pressure. The beast turned and took a round to the forehead. One of its eye's bulged as the back of its head erupted sending brain matter and bits of skull flying out over the pavement. The monster fell dead.

Two more ragers charged forward. Tibbs ignored the screams of George and Levi and kept firing. He knew as soon as they were dead, the beasts would turn to him next.

Corey ripped up the hood of the truck and charged Chad. Hot rounds struck the shield and went through it, but it was nearly impossible for Chad to determine where the monster's head was. He hopped into the back seat. Low on ammo, he would make them climb into the cab to get him. He could defend Katie there, and create a make shift bottleneck. It was about the best possible kill zone he could create. The army taught him to fight against conventional enemies using conventional tactics. At this point, all training other than shooting was out the window.

Corey leapt to the driver's side of the large truck. His weight collapsed the running board. Soon, he would kill the little people inside.

Brian looked down at his empty weapon. He tossed it into the grass of the dark Missouri night and turned on the Warthog. One of the ragers was trying to get at the injured little girl. He tromped the gas and the truck roared to life. Dirt and rocks kicked up behind its tires. It bounced half into the ditch before Brian jerked the wheel to the shoulder. He was lined up to ram the beast.

Apis charged the Warthog and rammed his heavy bony skull into the truck. Brian felt a tremendous force on his driver's side. The Warthog was knocked sideways and rammed into the rear quarter panel, missing Corey. Hot searing pain tore through Brian's body. The bull's horn had penetrated the door and ripped open his side. He could see one of his rib bones protruding from his shirt. Hot sticky blood emptied onto his pants and legs. He felt himself drifting away. Apis dipped his head and jerked it up. The thick powerful neck muscles flexed, sending the truck on its side. Sights and sounds of the battle started to drift away from Brian. They seemed so far away from him. He knew he was dying. And then he knew darkness.

Corey turned to see Apis save him from the truck. His focus went to the driver. Corey leapt from the side the truck to the Warthog. He tore off the driver's side door and pulled Brian's body out and started smashing it against the side of the truck. Blood and gore squirted out with each slam, and bits of flesh and bone tore away. Corey tossed the ragged corpse into the tall grass of the ditch before turning his attention to the front of the caravan where two of his ragers were locked in battle with some sort of large metal suit that had a man inside.

One of the ragers turned to Tibbs. He fired his pistol until it was empty and then he threw it at the beast. He picked up a piece of the handle bar of Terry's four wheeler and stood like a baseball played, "Come on, you ugly mother fuckers!"

James Fipps stepped from around the back of the truck in

his ORB suit. It was about eight foot tall, a little shorter than an emperor rager, but much larger than the ones here on the street. The arms had one hydraulic at each joint allowing it to move. It was made of quarter inch steel and the cockpit area was covered in a roll bar with thick welded grating protecting the pilot. The right hand had a ditch digger chain saw attached to the outside of the forearm that moved independently of a smaller three prong claw hand. It that ran the entire length of the forearm. The left hand had a three jack hammers surrounding the forearm that retracted and extended beyond a large two prong claw.

"Get behind me, boys!" Fipps growled, a little cigar in his mouth that shook when he spoke. "Let me show you how ORBS handle these bitches!"

The two beasts turned and charged. Fipps cranked down on a lever and four thick metal hydraulic support posts slammed into the ground on all directions. The first rager collided against the sergeant. The clawed hand grabbed the beast around the shoulder. He flipped a lever and the claw pinched down and the chain saw roared to life. The second beasts shouldered into Fipps, and but the hydraulic supports flexed under the force of the blow and quickly pressed back, righting the sergeant and keeping him upright. The beasts snarled and futilely punched the battle suit, ignoring the pain and gore that ripped through its body as the saw cut off its arm at the shoulder. Great gouts of blood and gore sprayed out from the wound. The rager immediately grew weaker from loss of blood, but Sargent Fipps knew it would recover quickly. The second monster ignored the thick two pronged claw that grabbed its waist and instead shredded its fingers trying to rip off the thick grating protecting the sarge.

Fipps pulled down on another lever and pushed a button on the panel in front of him. The wounded rager was hoisted in the air. It weakly kicked, but Fipps knew it would regenerate blood soon.

The other rager managed to get a grip on one of the grates protecting him and bent it up, nearly pulling it off. Fipps activated the jackhammers. They extended into the chest of the rager. The beast snarled and screamed in pain. In seconds, the jack hammers pulverized the chest of the beast, spilling hot bloody entrails of the dying monster onto the pavement. Fipps slammed another lever, and the three prong claw on the right hand rotated the first beast. He lowered the chain saw again, this time it cut off its head. He let both monsters go and raised his four support stanchions back up. The machine hummed and Sergeant Fipps started toward the rest of the group.

Levi skidded his ZRV sideways, "Get on!" He yelled to George. George jumped on the back. Levi picked both feet up and they sped off toward Branson.

"What about the others?" George yelled through the heavy wind blowing past his face.

"I tried the radio, got nothing. Our only chance is to get the fuck out of here."

A tall, lanky, rager leapt on the hood of the truck. Even as thin as it was, the beast's weight collapsed the thin metal under it. Shane fired rounds through the windshield. The glass spider webbed until it was clouded over with cracks. Shane retreated back with Chad and Katie.

"Just wait for it," Chad counted rounds in his magazine. "No point in wasting ammo."

The rager stabbed her hands into the glass and grabbed the top of the truck's cab. Bright red blood dripped down briefly from the cuts in her hand. Growling, she peeled back the top of the cab like a sardine can. Chad nonchalantly lifted his rifle and fired a single shot. The hot lead tore through the rager's face. Her eyes bulged cross-eyed from the gas compression in her skull and she fell dead. Her heavy form half landing in the cab and half landing on the hood.

Corey turned to see the large mechanical man charging him. It was covered in blood and gore. Rage filled him. He grabbed the bumper of the Warthog and pulled. The truck lurched toward him. Corey placed his foot up on the driver's side fender and jerked the bumper as hard as he could. His thick muscles flexed and strained. Gouts of puss from the necrotic tissue covering his body popped and bubbled, dripping long streams of thick yellow cream down his body. The bumper popped and it was ripped free.

Apis rushed passed, the mighty golden bull lowered its head and crashed headlong into the ORB. Sargent Fipps swung his ditch saw down, cutting a deep swath into the bull as he was knocked from his feet. He tumbled into the ditch, landing face down in the grass. He quickly regained his battle suit's feet and locked down his stanchions. The ditch embankments would make him steadier than ever.

Corey hit a full sprint and leapt from the ditch into the air. He grabbed the bumper with both hands and brought it down over his head. Sargent Fipps raised his left clawed hand to shield himself from the blow. The metallic club came down hard. It took off one of the hooks before smashing into the cab of the suit. The blow bent in the strong roll bars protecting Sargent Fipps and Corey's weight crashed into the machine, bending one of the stanchions, but it did not topple over.

Sargent Fipps jabbed forward with his pneumatic jackhammers. The spike tipped hammers pounded into Corey's chest, pulverizing his flesh and sending out splatters of blood and gore.

Sammy popped the trunk on Scout-1. She tossed two

tactical bags over each shoulder and grabbed the long black case holding her sniper rifle. She ran across the street and started up the hill. She turned and surveyed the scene. Most of the ragers lay dead. Corey was fighting the ORB suit and Apis was recovering from the ditch digger shoulder wound. She didn't dare lose Corey or Apis. The others were replaceable. She closed her eyes for a brief moment and turned to run back up the hill. She would come back later and kill them. ...She would kill all of ZOD.

Tibbs ran to Terry, giving the hulking mechanical monstrosity a quick glance in awe as it slowly stepped by. Pulling Terry out from under the twisted metal of his ZRV, he was happy to find him alive. Terry was barely conscious and a trickle of bright red blood dripped from the corner of his mouth. "Come on, Terry. You gotta make it!" Tibbs gently lowered Terry's unconscious form downone the pavement. He felt relief watching the few ragers run up the embankment and disappear into the forest.

Sargent Fipps limped his ORB to the back of the loader truck. "We need to get back to base, pronto."

Shane pulled up alongside in the large damaged diesel truck. The right rear quarter panel was caved in, and was rubbing the tire, but he hoped it could make the short drive. "All the fuel is on the back on this truck. We won't run out."

Chad slid his rifle over his shoulder and climbed down from the truck, "Any other survivors?"

Tibbs nodded, "Terry is still alive, but he won't last long. I'll stay behind and put him down. ...I've done it before."

"You need to just do it now and get it over with." Chris opened the door to Scout-1. "Nothing good comes from putting it off. I can do it if you need."

"No, I got this. I owe it to Terry. We have been through a lot together."

"Fair enough," Chris nodded his head slowly.

Artez did a quick ammo check and policed the bodies for spare ammo as they placed them in the back of the loader truck next to the ORB.

Chris took a deep breath before getting into Scout-1. He drove next to Tibbs and handed him a first aid kit. "Here, this was Sarah's. Use it to make Terry comfortable before he passes—just in case you struggle with it. But, don't stay too long. Those ragers could be back."

"Thanks."

Shane, and the other's drove off, leaving Tibbs with one of the undamaged ZRVs. He cradled Terry's head and scooted under him. Terry came to and winced before smiling, "Guess this is it, huh Mister Rapper guy?"

Tibbs felt a sting in his nose and a watery tear that streaked down his cheek. "I think so, brolo. It was one hell of a ride," he fought back tears.

"You know I can't wait too long. The ragers will be back."

"That's why it's you, then?" Terry coughed and grimaced, "Because you put down Jeff and Nish?"

Tibbs fought to hide the pain and surprise that Terry knew. "Maybe... maybe I just wanted to pay you some respect and not leave you here on the cold ass pavement like a discarded hammer."

Terry smiled, "Careful, you're liable to feel feelings."

Tibbs chuckled and patted his shoulder. He popped open the first aid kit and thumbed through it. "I think I can patch you up a bit and stay with you a while."

"Okay then, Mister Rapper boy. I died years ago, before the fall. I had to kill my deer."

"Deer?"

"It's nothing, brolo. It's time to..." Terry's jaw went slack and his body went limp. His chest rose and fell but his friend had slipped into unconsciousness.

Tibbs sobbed. It was the first time since the collapse he allowed himself to cry. He cried for his daughters, he cried for Jeff and Nish, and now he cried for Terry. *Fuck this fucking world!* He rummaged through the first aid kit and he found a syringe labeled AOE 293. *Sammy's Blood*, Tibbs thought to himself. He glanced down at Terry and the pistol in his hand.

Did he want to kill another friend? Would he lose the last shred of his humanity? He couldn't just leave him to die if he couldn't bring himself to kill him. Maybe Sammy's blood would heal him? She didn't turn into a monster like the others. Tibbs wiped the tears from his eyes and took the cap off of the needle. He stared at the red glowing blood in the syringe. How would he administer it? Vein? He wasn't sure he could hit it. The muscle? Would it get in the blood stream? Tibbs shook his head and took a deep breath. The needle wasn't very long, but he hoped it would reach. Raising the needle and syringe above his head, he took a deep breath and stabbed down as hard as he could. His thumb pressed the plunger and injected the tainted blood. Seconds turned into minutes and Terry slowly drifted off. His heart beat became fainter and fainter until Tibbs could feel it no longer.

Tibbs stood up and gave Terry a last look before getting on his ZRV.

Sammy exhaled slowly with her finger on her trigger. She watched Tibbs through the scope of her long rifle. She slowly depressed the trigger. The rifle lurched in her arms. The single crack echoed across the valley. Tibbs's head exploded in a bright mist of red blood. His body collapsed over the front of the ZRV. Sammy smiled and stood. She slung her rifle over her shoulder and patted Corey on the shoulder. "Five to go, big guy. Five to go."

Dear Reader,

I want to thank you for taking the time to read *The Apocalypse of Enoch* series! I thought this would be a great format to tell you some behind the scenes truths about this series.

In 2011 I wrote a small short story for a comic anthology press (now defunct) called *IHero Entertainment*. The owner recognized my growing popularity in the business and was eager to get me to write on one of their comics. They had some greats in the business like Tom Waltz—editor at IDW and Sean Taylor of *Gene Simmons Dominatrix* comic and *House of Horrors*. I tried to back out, citing I knew very little of 'super hero' lit. The owner was not taking no for an answer. I wrote a quick little story about a woman who had one power, to turn invisible. The story opens in Saint Louis the day after she had been hired to assassinate a doomsday cult trying to bring about a zombie apocalypse. I won't give you any spoilers in case some of you hard core fans find an out of print copy of it, but the story was well received.

About eight months later, the owner of New Babel Books (an accomplished writer in his own right) read the story and contacted me to write a zombie thriller for his company. I had zero interest in writing a zombie thriller. There are so many plot holes in a zombie story, the mere thought of writing one sent me into fits. The owner was disappointed, but understood.

Several months later (around late June) I was eating with my wife at this upscale restaurant in my home town called "Wang Gangs" (Yes, it really is upscale. Food is legit!) and we were talking about the Rapture. Granted, I was aware the word rapture doesn't even appear in the Christian bible, but I argued what if it didn't even take the whole body when it happened? I asked my wife what if it was unlike the popular idea of the entire body disappearing and instead only the soul was lost. My wife chuckled and said, "Well, they would just be like zombies."

I can honestly say the entire plot for the first book hit me like a punch in the fun bag. I started writing on napkins and was STILL outlining on my phone on the way home. I phoned New Babel Books the next day to see if they had filled that contract. The owner told me that not only had they not filled it, all the writers they solicited for it, told them the same thing I did—the traditional zombie story sucked. I pitched my idea, he said he loved it and wanted a proposal. I wrote it up and sent it that night.

I got the email back, but there was a catch... New Babel Books wanted it for an early 2012 launch which means that wanted the completed manuscript in their inbox by August 30th. ...just 60 days away.

I had next to no time to write this! Not only had I never written a horror novel before, I had never wrote a novel in less than six months. Yet, in my excited state, I foolishly took the project.

The first thing I did was sign on two medical doctors to help me learn the biology of the viral aspect. They were Josh Poos and Sheree Speckman. Next, I enlisted two ordained leaders—one that wished to remain anonymous and the other was James Gotcher.

I started writing at Starbucks. From open to close, seven days a week. I spent more time researching that the first week than writing. I had no words completed and my character bible was so weak, I dared not outline. There was no way I was going to be able to complete this project if I did not come up with a faster method. So, I did what no one had ever done before (that I knew of), I took REAL people and wrote them in as themselves. My first character was Shane Nettleton. While he really is a three time Iraq tour veteran, he is not, nor has he ever, been on trial for war crimes. But, it seemed like a fun character twist. The others were true to form. I needed an EMT, so I asked Ryan Roach to be a character and so on and so forth. When I needed a news caster, I reached to April

Simpson of FOX 2. She had survived a brain tumor when the doctors told her she was going to die. She was as tough as she was beautiful and when she accepted my proposal to be in the series, I excitedly bragged to social media that I got her to be in it. This led to my actor friends to express interest to be in the story as well, such as Matt Hill (Teenage Mutant Ninja Turtles/ Ed, Edd, and Eddy) and Peter Mayhew (Chewbacca from Star Wars) just to name a few. This led to some tough challenges to try and seamlessly blend them into the story without it seeming contrived.

I think it's safe to surmise that if you are reading this thank you letter, I did a fair job writing book one and blending the actors in the best I could. Some fans always ask how long it took me... well, it was 59 days and 18 hours when I hit submit in the email from when I took the contract.

I have included the beginning of *The Apocalypse of Enoch's* first ever spin off, *Dark Harvest* by Edward Gehlert. He has taken a no holds barred approach to my world and spun a tale the both of us think you're going to love! Just remember one of my favorite quotes:

"If success were easy, everyone would be having it."

Thanks for all the support,

Shane Moore

THE APOCALYPSE OF ENOCH

CHILDREN OF ENOCH
BY
EDWARD GEHLERT

A NEW BABEL BOOKS RELEASE

"For I have chosen him, that he may command his children and his household after him to keep the way of the Lord by doing righteousness and justice, so that the Lord may bring to Abraham what he has promised him."

Genesis 18:19

1
STICKS & STONES

Hannibal, Missouri – Seven Years Ago

Joey and his younger brother Sean ambled along the banks of the Mississippi River enjoying the weather. The smell of the water energized the young boys while they played. As the temperature gradually warmed, they had been able to convince their mother they didn't need to wear windbreakers anymore. She grudgingly gave them permission to remove the jackets, only forcing them to put the apparel on because of the cold snap that slipped in that morning anyway.

Joey tied his jacket around his waist; giving him full use of his arms and hands to poke and prod his younger brother. Sean had initially tied his jacket as well, but when his brother started aggravating him he used it as a makeshift defense against the abuse. He did his best to dodge his older brother's mistreatment and occasionally managed to avoid some of the torment. Joey cuffed him on the side of his head with his jacket with enough force to cause his head to turn. From his new field of vision Sean noticed a strange pile of rocks further down the trail. He tossed his jacket it to his mom with wild abandon before running up to investigate.

Joey raced after his brother when he bolted away, snatching up a stick from the ground as he went. He swung it back and forth a few times and when he got close to his brother he began poking him in the back with it. Sean was completely engrossed in examining the strange pile and didn't seem to notice what Joey was doing for a few seconds.

"Momma, make him stop!"

"Momma, make him stop," teased Joey, though he did pull the stick away from his brother when he noticed the glare his mother gave him.

Mary shook her head as she watched her sons bicker back and forth. She was a young mother, having gotten pregnant with Joey when she was sixteen and had him just a month shy of her seventeenth birthday. She ended up marrying his father shortly after the boy's second birthday.

He had proposed to her when they found out that she was pregnant with another child after Joey turned just over a year old. She had lost the baby a few months into the pregnancy, but the young couple decided to go ahead with the marriage anyway. After all, they were in love and had a bright future.

"Momma, come see!" squealed Sean with excitement, breaking her out of her thoughts.

"What is it, Hun?"

"It's just a pile of sticks and rocks!" called out Joey from beside his brother.

Mary chuckled and moved toward her sons. Sean had always been excitable and so full of wonder with the world around him. It was nice to see that he hadn't lost any of that fascination after celebrating his sixth birthday earlier in the month.

When she looked at her youngest boy, and especially when she looked into those bright green eyes of his, she always felt a little out of place and uneasy. She loved him, that was certain, but when she had originally found out she was pregnant with him she had seriously considered having an abortion.

The timing of her pregnancy had been all wrong. Things had soured between her and Doug, the boy's father. When she found out he was cheating on her, she decided to return the favor. After a few months of both of them sneaking around on each other, Mary had decided to call it quits.

The day she was going to meet the lawyer to file paperwork was the same day morning sickness hit her. She couldn't remember how long she had cried when the test she took came back positive, but she did remember the angry look Doug gave her and the heated words.

They both decided to stick it out until after the baby was born and paternity was proven. If it was his they would try to reconcile and, if not, the divorce would certainly proceed. During that time, things had become so cold around the house that Mary kept entertaining the idea of abortion just so she could get away from Doug. Even little Joey knew that something was wrong between Momma and Daddy.

She felt guilty every time she thought about how much she almost had given up, and at times like this when Sean smiled up at her and moved his red hair out of his eyes, she felt choked up.

"Show Momma what you found," she said, managing to keep the catch out of her throat.

"I told you it's just a pile of sticks and rocks, Mom," Joey said under his breath.

"Nuh-uh Joey, it's something special. Someone made it," countered Sean.

Mary knelt down and examined the pile her son had found. She noticed that the rocks were all different shapes and sizes and it looked like the sticks had been placed in an 'x'pattern between the various layers of rocks and dirt.

"This wasn't here last week," she remarked.

"No, it wasn't. I would of 'membered," Sean said proudly.

"Who cares? It's just a stupid pile of dirt and rocks," his older brother said while stepping on Sean's foot.

"Momma, he's getting my shoe dirty!"

Mary wasn't listening to the bickering of her children anymore. The size of the pile is what intrigued her most. It was roughly three foot high and had a diameter of at least five feet. The placement of the sticks, small branches really, started at the base of the mound and contained another cross section in the middle with one more on top. The top branches were tied together with what appeared to be hair.

The smell of freshly dug earth was heavy in the air and there was another odor, very faint, that Mary couldn't place. The wind picked up, causing a chill to run all over her body and she hugged Sean's windbreaker closer to her chest. The sound of the wind moving among the fall trees made an eerie wail that sent a shudder through her spine. A shudder that intensified when she realized that, other than the wind and the ripples on the shore of the Mississippi, there was no other noises coming from the forest.

"Momma?" she heard Sean ask.

"Put your jackets back on," she said as she handed Sean his windbreaker.

"But—" began Joey.

"No 'buts' now. Get your jacket back on, we're goin' home," she said with a tone of finality.

"We can't dig in the pile?" asked Sean, sounding disappointed.

Mary felt a sense of dread when he asked her that question. The thought of disturbing the pile really bothered her, although she had no idea why. She could also tell that Joey didn't want to have anything more to do with it when she saw the look on his face.

"Sean, that would be stupid, we have no idea what could be in there," said the older child trying to sound mad, but failing to hide the look of unease on his face from his mother. Something about the pile was making his mother scared to be close to it and that made him nervous. He hastily put his jacket on and looked at his mother.

"No, Hun, we're not going to dig in the dirt today," Mary began, "We don't have time for it. Your grandparents are going to be at the house this afternoon and Momma needs to clean."

"Okay, Momma," Sean said with all traces of disappointment gone when he heard his grandparents were going to be visiting.

"Well, we better get moving," Mary said as she ushered her children away from the mysterious mound.

The wind began blowing again and Joey zipped up his jacket as he walked. Mary pulled out a scarf and wrapped it around her neck to keep the bitter bite of the wind away from her skin. Sean skipped along happily, occasionally glancing back in the direction of the mound.

Mary reached down and held her boys hands as they headed back home. Neither she nor Joey noticed Sean waving behind them to the old, scraggly bearded man that had crested the small rise next to the rock pile.

"Oh Lord, thy will be done," panted the old man, his thick Cajun accent even more muffled as he walked up the small hill with his arms full of rocks. Sweat rolled off his beard and eyebrows in a constant stream and he could feel a hard pressure in his back, a dull ache that seemed to have gotten worse with every step he took.

He felt a moment of panic as he saw the woman and two kids walking away from his newest cairn. He nearly dropped his load until he saw the smallest boy look back at him, smile and then wave. For a brief moment the old man felt more peace than he had in the past year, even the pain in his back subsided. The child was the first person to acknowledge his presence since he had started his journey. The old man smiled and nodded toward the boy.

When the family was out of sight he carefully placed a layer of rocks around the top edge of the cairn, he then found two large sticks that were roughly the same size as each other. He pulled out his knife and cut off enough of his beard to tie the small branches together.

After the sticks were tied he pulled out a carefully folded cloth from his front right pants pocket. This was the part that he hated the most, he knew he couldn't look in the cloth even though he knew he had to have been the one to place whatever item it contained in its folds.

He knew he couldn't look, and he knew he would never remember what it was. That was just the way it had been for this past year, ever since he had gotten what he called "The Thing."

It was "The Thing" that had compelled him to leave his family in New Orleans and travel up the banks of the Mississippi River, and to places beyond, to build these damn rock piles. It was also "The Thing" that kept him from remembering what he was putting in them.

He placed the folded cloth on the cross section of the sticks and began filling the area in with dirt and rocks. Once he had the mound completed to his liking he slowly set off to the north, following the banks of the river as he had done for so many months.

"Oh Lord, when you gonna' let 'ole Abi go on home?" He drawled over and over again wearily.

He tried to whistle but his mouth was too dry to make any notes. He felt parched, actually more thirsty than he could ever remember being before in his life.

His feet carried him close to the edge of the water and a strange calm came over him. He knelt down next to the river and saw his haggard reflection staring back at him from the muddy river.

He watched in fascination as his image became less weathered and started smiling at him, all the while seeming to get younger. The muddiness of the water slowly faded away and he could see himself wearing robes so white they almost shone with their own light.

He suddenly felt as though the weight of one the cairns was on his chest and he couldn't breathe. He felt himself falling forward and the cold waters of the river covering him up. He felt the waters dragging him down into darkness. A darkness that was suddenly driven away by the most beautiful light he had ever seen.

It would be two weeks before the body of Adolphe Billadeau, Abi to his friends and family, would be found in the Mississippi River just north of New Orleans. His family would hold a small funeral service for him, closed casket of course due to the decay and bloating of the body.

Those that knew him could only shake their heads in confusion and would never understand what had caused such a devoutly religious man to abandon them a year ago without a word of explanation.

THE APOCALYPSE OF ENOCH

If you asked anyone at the factory they would tell you Doug Tyler had always been a man that wasn't afraid of hard work. He would pull a double shift without batting an eye and would happily take any overtime that was offered.

He liked his job, it more than provided for his family, but the sad fact of the matter was that Doug Tyler didn't like his family very much. He would never admit it of course, just like he would never admit the reason he took all the extra shifts was so that he could stay away from them.

When he worked a half day on Saturday, he would stop in at one of the bars in town before heading home. Doug and a few coworkers would normally enjoy some drinks and then go their separate ways. Today was different. Today he was drinking alone.

Doug heard some news earlier in the day about Charlie Miller, a former classmate, who had just signed a deal to work for a major news company as a foreign correspondent. Doug's dream had always been to work in the news and when Mary ended up pregnant...

Doug slammed his glass down on the counter of the bar and motioned for the bartender, Derek, to fill it again.

"Slow down man," Derek said as he poured another gin and tonic, "Mary is going to kick your ass if you come home drunk again."

"Fuck Mary!" Doug hissed as he took the glass from Derek.

"Whoa man," Derek said, "I didn't know things were bad at home. I was just jokin' aroun'."

"I ain't mad at you, I'm mad at... At just shit!" Doug downed his drink and wiped his mouth with his sleeve. "My life could've been something. I could've been something."

Derek looked at Doug for a few seconds before he responded, "You are something. You're a husband and a father. Man, that has got to be the best thing in the world."

Doug snorted, "Yeah, it's fucking great! Family keeping me in this shithole of a' town, wife always bitching I ain't never spending enough time with them. Real paradise, man."

Doug motioned for Derek to fill his glass again and the barkeep took the container and placed it behind the counter, "I think you've had enough for today. Why don't you go on home, Doug?"

Doug looked at Derek and glanced at the liquors on the shelf behind him. He licked his lips as he slowly stood up and pulled out his wallet. He took a twenty dollar bill out and tossed it on the counter angrily, "Keep the change, fucker! It's the last dollar I'm gonna' ever spend in this shithole again! Won't give me booze? I'll hit another fuckin' dive!"

Derek took the money and put it in the cash register as Doug left his bar. He watched him walk away and didn't see him staggering too much. He thought briefly about how mad Doug seemed to be and chalked it up as everyone having a bad day now and again.

Derek tended to the other customers and, after a little while, all thoughts of Doug and his troubles were completely out of his mind. He would most likely be back in next week and Derek would have a talk with him then about his attitude.

Derek went about his job as if everything was right in the world.

"Gampy!" Sean squealed as soon as the old man came through the door.

Bradley Knox barely had time to brace himself before he was suddenly dealing with all the energetic love a six year old could throw at him. As he picked his grandson up he held him at arm's length and eyed the boy with mock seriousness.

"Think you can just hug me any time you want, huh?" said Bradley as he tossed the boy on the couch in front of him, "Well, take that!"

Sean giggled and laughed as his grandfather began tickling him. He tried countering the tickles with a few kicks and was making some progress with defending himself when his grandmother came in the door.

"Bradley!" She yelled, "What on God's good Earth do you think you are doing? The doctor told you to take it easy!"

Bradley stopped his assault long enough to glare at his wife, "Katie, if I can't play with my grandkids than what the hell good is it to keep on livin'?" He then proceeded about his task with renewed vigor, Sean laughing all the while.

Katie rolled her eyes as she took off her coat, "You stubborn ass. Let's just wait and see what your daughter has to say to you."

"And what am I going to say?" came Mary's voice from the top of the staircase.

Looking up towards the sound of her voice, Bradley saw the picture of Jesus he had given her as a housewarming gift. He was so proud when Katie and he had sold the house to her and Doug. He was just as proud now when he saw the picture prominently displayed above the second floor landing. His baby girl came around the corner with a smile on her face and rushed down the stairs to hug him.

"Dad, Mom, it's great to see you! How's life in Florida treating you?"

Bradley was about to speak but was interrupted by his wife, "It's beautiful down there. I was just telling your father that this summer you need to bring the kids down there for a visit. They would just love the beaches and we could all go sailing."

"Can we go, Momma'?" asked Sean.

Mary hugged her mother as she answered, "I don't know, Hun. We'll have to see if Daddy wants to go."

At the mention of her husband, Mary's mother stiffened in her embrace.

"He doesn't have to come along if he doesn't want to, Mare," she said, using Mary's childhood nickname.

"Of course he does, he's my husband," laughed Mary.

"He might be, but he, you know... He just doesn't act like it all the time," Katie said.

"What's Gamma' mean, Momma?" asked Sean.

"Go tell your brother to hurry up in the shower," Mary told Sean, her eyes never leaving her mother's face.

"But what does..."

"I said go!" shouted Mary.

Sean was so startled he jumped. His eyes started to tear up as he ran up the stairs calling his brother's name.

"Katie, there was no call for that!" Bradley scolded his wife, "What happened back then is back then... Now is now."

"Mom, why did you even bring that up?"

Katie looked at the two of them and her stern gaze slowly faded, "I'm sorry, I don't know what came over me."

"Mom, maybe you would like some tea. I have some in the icebox if you want to grab a glass."

"I'd like that. I'll get it myself," said Katie as she walked into the kitchen.

Mary moved close to her father and whispered, "It's getting worse isn't it?"

Bradley looked at his daughter and nodded his head, "I think this will be the last time we can visit when she will recognize everyone."

Mary felt a pang of sadness. Her mother had been diagnosed with the early stages of Alzheimer's about a year ago. The disease was steadily getting worse and she was prone to bouts of meanness. During these fits she would say the most hurtful things for no particular reason.

Her dad had warned her that her mother was turning into a completely different person and he was having trouble dealing with it. He had also hinted around that it would most likely be only a matter of time before his beloved Katie would have to be placed in an assisted living complex.

The whole reason behind moving to Florida in the first place was to find a nice retirement facility. One that would allow the couple to stay together while she was able to get the fulltime care she needed from professionals. Bradley had a dark suspicion that eventually she would get to a point where she would become violent. If that happened, there would be no way they could stay together.

"I am so sorry, Daddy," Mary said as she hugged her father, "You know I am here for anything that I can do to help."

Upstairs they could hear the sound of a door being slammed and some muffled conversation between the two boys.

"I know that, Mare," he said as he returned the hug, "But

you know there isn't much a young woman can do. Especially when she is so busy raising two growing boys."

They held on to each other for a few moments, finally able to share a moment with someone else who fully understood the pain they felt in their hearts concerning the troubles that were ahead.

Their hug was interrupted by a smiling Joey rushing down the stairs. His short, damp hair sticking up in places on his head gave Bradley the impression of a hedgehog that was half angry.

"Grampa!" the boy said as he pushed himself between his mother and Bradley.

"Heya' Joseph!"

The old man tried picking up his grandson and gave up after a brief moment. The boy had gotten so big since he had last seen him! Bradley stepped back and visually compared the boy's height against his mother.

"Wow, you are so big now! You are almost as tall as your mother!" the old man said.

Joey beamed proudly then asked, "Where's Grandma?"

"She's getting a dri—" began Mary when she was interrupted by a loud scream from the kitchen and the crashing of breaking glass.

After his outburst, Doug had felt a little ashamed. Derek had always treated him good and he didn't deserve the kind of attitude that Doug had laid on him. *I'll apologize Monday after work,* he thought as he pulled into the parking lot of another bar he had been to a few times.

Doug knew that Derek was right, he should just go on home, but he didn't feel like dealing with hearing Mary bitch about him drinking again. He had promised her a few months earlier he wouldn't drink anymore, a promise that was made as a direct result of a violent outburst by him.

He had been out late one Friday after work, drinking with

some of his friends. When he realized he was too drunk to drive he had called a cab to take him home. While waiting on the taxi he had a few more shots and one last beer.

He had been very drunk when he had gotten to the house. Mary met him at the door, demanding to know what the hell he was doing out so late. Doug couldn't remember the entire argument that followed, so he could never say for sure what had caused him to hit her.

All he knew was that when he had hit her, he had blackened her eye and it had felt good to do it. It was like all the years of frustration had come out in one rapid movement of his muscles. He wasn't proud of what happened, but he certainly didn't truly regret it either.

Doug shook away the memory, turned his car off and headed into the bar. Inside there was country playing, not his favorite music, but the singer was wailing something about lost dreams that caught his attention.

He stayed in the bar drinking and, with every sip he took, he became more sullen. The bartender finally had to threaten to call the police when Doug started verbally lashing out at the other patrons. Doug left in a tirade of foul language and with the promise to never lower himself to drink in such a rat-hole establishment again.

Driving home he ran a few stop signs that he didn't notice and he clipped the rear end of another vehicle that was parked up the block from where he lived. He stopped for just the briefest of moments and then, when he was fairly sure that no one had seen him, he drove around the corner.

He pulled his car into the alley behind his house, hoping he would be able to sneak inside without his wife or kids noticing he was home. If he could have seen himself through the eyes of any onlookers, especially the one whose car he had hit and was dialing 911, he would have laughed at the futility of his actions.

He thought he was moving with cat-like grace, but instead his movements were awkward and he stumbled more than walked. More than once he had to stop and use the fence as a makeshift crutch to keep from falling over.

He stopped halfway to the back door and looked around at

his yard. The kids had left their bikes against the inside of the fence instead of putting them in the garage again. There was also a scattered assortment of other toys on the lawn, toys he could only vaguely remember getting them.

"Damn kids don't respec' nuttin'," he mumbled as continued his drunken surveillance of the backyard.

He worked his way to the door and fished around in his pockets for the keys, when he couldn't find them he pulled out his hunting knife and began fiddling with the lock.

He was actually surprised when the door opened and it took him a bit of time to recover from the sudden swing of fortune. He walked in the house and decided to grab a quick bite of food before sneaking upstairs.

He turned around the corner to go into his kitchen when a loud, wailing scream erupt right in front of him. He felt something hit him on the head and he instinctively lashed out with his arm to protect himself.

He felt just a small amount of resistance on the blade of the knife he was still holding and then something warm and sticky splashed on his face and arm. He tried focusing on the scene before him, but through whatever was burning his eyes and what had hit him on the head, it was hard to concentrate. He heard a strange sound, as if one of his kids was sliding across the floor, but then another sound made him snap to attention.

"Katie!" he heard a familiar male voice scream from the direction of the living room.

Doug turned to face the new sound when his vision cleared just enough for him to recognize his mother-in-law lying on the floor. Her eyes were open wide with terror and she was feebly trying to stop the flow of blood that was pouring from her neck. For some reason the image struck him as funny.

Something inside of him snapped. All the weight of his worries, his failures and the thought of everyone doing better than him suddenly hit him all at once. He knew, on some level of rational thought, that laughing was wrong in this situation. No matter how hard he tried though, he couldn't stop smiling as he looked down at the old bitch. Years of frustration came out in the form of a kick to her head as his father-in-law ran screaming into the kitchen.

Katie felt bad about the things she had said, even as she realized it wasn't really her fault. She knew she was sick and that there was nothing that could be done for her. Oh how she wished the disease wouldn't make her so mean sometimes!

She was taking her time in the kitchen and had already enjoyed a few sips of her tea. She was trying to calm down enough to go back in the living room when she heard a rustling at the backdoor.

I left the cat outside again, she thought to herself, *Why do I keep doing that?*

Katie stood up and headed towards the backdoor of her house. She saw a man come through the door with a knife in his hand and her heart froze. She backed away slowly a few steps as her mind raced for something to do.

When the man suddenly stumbled in front of her all she could do was scream and hit him in the head with the heavy glass mug that held her iced tea. She thought she actually might have knocked him senseless when his head first dropped low and his knees buckled. She had taken a step toward him, thinking she could push him over and call the cops, when he lashed out at her with the knife.

For just the briefest of moments she thought the man had missed her, until she tried to scream again and nothing came out but a wet gurgle. That's when the searing pain in her throat began. She reached up to check the wound when she felt blood saturating her blouse. She felt thick fluid pumping through her hand as she tried to stop the bleeding.

She slid against the countertop, her polyester clothing creating an eerie low screeching sound, until she was stretched out on the floor. She stared up at the intruder and was surprised to see that it was Doug. Only it didn't really look like Doug. His eyes were so hollow looking and he seemed to be staring right through her. The thing that terrified her most about him was the deranged smile he had on his face.

THE APOCALYPSE OF ENOCH

She heard Bradley yell for her and she tried again to yell out, this time a warning, but again the only sound that she could make was a gurgle. She started coughing and realized that her lungs were filling up with fluid. In horror she understood that she was choking on her own blood.

The pain in her neck started to subside a little, and sounds seemed to be coming from far away. She felt something warm running down her legs and hoped she hadn't peed herself. Doug continued to stare at her with that crazy smile of his until the door to the living room flew open and Bradley came running in.

She smiled up at her husband and then she knew only darkness when her son-in-law snapped her neck with one quick and forceful kick to the side of her head.

Bradley couldn't believe his eyes when he entered the kitchen, the scene before him was too surreal to even begin processing. His beloved Katie, wife and companion for forty-five years, was lying in a fast spreading pool of blood and his son-in-law was holding a bloody knife and smiling at him.

"No!" the old man yelled as Doug kicked Katie in the head, as casually as if he were getting a piece of garbage away from his shoe.

Bradley charged at Doug and swung a right cross with all the force his rage could summon. He missed as the younger man ducked under the blow and came up with the point of the knife leading the way into his stomach.

The old man let out a gasp of air as he felt his legs go numb and fall out from underneath him. He realized he was being held up by Doug and the damn knife that was sticking in his gut. He let out a scream when Doug twisted the knife and began to saw back and forth while pulling up on the weapon, the smile never leaving his face.

Bradley's arms lost all strength and he swooned momentarily, when he regained his senses he realized he was on the floor next to his wife. He didn't know how he had gotten there or how he had managed to move his arms, but now they were busy holding in his entrails. The smell of feces and urine was all around him and he started gagging. He looked at the blood stained face of his wife and couldn't fight the tears that started to flow as he stared into her lifeless eyes.

"Run, Mare!" he tried to scream but the words came out barely above a whisper, "Get the kids and run!"

Doug stepped over his legs and entered the living room, roughly pulling his foot away from some of Bradley's insides it had gotten tangled with. Bradley heard Mary and Joey scream and then the sound of footsteps running up the stairs and someone beating on the front door.

The old man still couldn't feel his legs and he wondered if Bradley had severed some nerves in his spine when he first stuck him. More screams came from upstairs and the beating on the front door turned into a crashing sound. He tried to crawl towards the living room but he just didn't have the strength to move any more.

He was getting weaker by the second and he knew he was dying, he knew that as surely as he had known anything in his life. His thoughts drifted to Mary when she was a baby and when he and Katie had first brought her home from the hospital.

His mind played out a few more memories, the happiest ones in his life, and his vision slowly faded. He fought it for as long as he could and when he saw his wife looking down at him with a sad smile on her beautiful young face, he knew he couldn't fight anymore.

"Take me home, Katie," he whispered.

The image of his wife bent down and lovingly stroked his face. When she gently kissed him on his forehead all the pain suddenly vanished and he only knew joy.

Mary had no idea what was going on in the kitchen, but she

was even more terrified when she heard her father's scream. Joey had grabbed her arm and was shaking and she had begun to subconsciously rub the back of his head. When the door opened and Doug stepped out they both started to breathe a sigh of relief, until they saw all the blood on him and the twisted smile on his face.

"Oh God!" Mary screamed as she pushed Joey in front of her towards the stairs.

Her son made a strange gurgling sound but ran as fast as he could. As the pair neared the bottom of the staircase there was a loud banging on the door, the sudden sound causing Mary's heart to leap even higher in her chest. Without looking she bolted up the stairs, all the while pushing her son in front of her and listening to the strange sound Joey was making.

Doug was right behind her and struck out at her twice, once slashing the back of his wife's neck. If she felt his strike connect she gave no indication of it and continued her sprint up the stairs.

Doug had heard the banging and he was surprised to see, through one of the small side windows on the front door as he ran past, two policemen standing on his front porch. It looked like one had just recovered from a kick and the next one was lining up to try to break the door down.

I don't have a lot of time, Doug thought as he ran up the stairs after his wife and eldest child, *They ruined my life... They need to pay!*

Mary was at the top of the stairs and turned just long enough to throw down a small end table at him, the one his mother had left him after she had died. Doug's anger was doubled when the cheap wooden table flew over his head and he heard it smash against the wall.

"Daddy, stop!" wailed Joey, "We'll be good!"

Mary had moved in front of the boy, who had fallen and seamed to be frozen with fear. She was waving her arms in front of her, as if making the motion for him to go away would work. The cut on her neck had caused blood to spread over the shoulders of her shirt, the sight of it made Doug smile wider.

He stepped forward and slashed at her, cutting her on the inside of her right arm. She gasped in pain and then continued screaming. There was a loud cracking sound from the front door and the sound of glass shattering.

"Police!" yelled a new voice echoing up the stairs.

Doug snarled like a wild animal and grabbed his wife by the top of her hair. She screamed even louder when he pulled her closer to him and stabbed upward with his knife, ripping into her flesh just below her left lung.

"No!" Joey yelled and flung himself up from the floor towards his dad.

Doug yanked the knife out of Mary's tender skin while pushing her to the ground away from him. Joey made it a few steps before his father hit him in the temple with the handle of his knife, using a backhand strike. The young boy crumpled over the side of the staircase and made a sickening *thud* when he landed on the hardwood floor below.

"Joey!" Mary wailed.

She started crawling down the staircase, her eyes focused on her oldest son lying on his back and moaning. She noticed that the side window on the door had been busted out and a crack was across the center of it. Through the now glassless window she saw a police officer pointing a gun.

A loud explosion ripped through the living room as the officer shot his gun at Doug. The deranged man felt something zip by his head as he bent down to plunge the knife into Mary's back.

She moaned a few times, but continued to crawl down the stairs towards her wounded son. Doug was relentless with his strikes and she felt each plunge of the knife as it entered her body. There would be a small numbness until the blade was pulled free and stuck back in.

She was staring at her son when the blade of the knife pierced her in the back of the head. The last image her living mind would ever hold was that of Joey staring vacantly up at her.

There was another loud explosion as the officer fired his weapon again. This time the shot hit Doug in his left shoulder and it spun him around. He was a few steps from the top of the stairs and the picture of Jesus was staring down at him. In Doug's mind he was already judging his soul.

He was so intent on the image of Christ that he almost overlooked his youngest son, who had been showering while the horrible massacre was taking place, staring down at him.

Doug reached out and grabbed Sean, who offered no resistance, and pulled him close. He turned his son around and placed the knife on the boy's neck. He had just started to put pressure on the blade when the officer fired his gun again.

Sean didn't know what was happening; he had heard all the screaming and hid in the bathroom. When he heard the gunshots he came out and saw blood all over the hallway. He walked over to check on his father and froze when he saw his mother lying still with blood still oozing from cuts on her back.

His father grabbed him and turned him around. It seemed he was being turned very slowly and then he felt the knife at his throat. He wasn't so much scared as he was thankful he wasn't looking his dad in the eyes anymore. His father wasn't in there, it was something else. Something that was dark and evil.

His father suddenly let him go when another loud bang echoed up from downstairs, although the knife did cut him very deeply from his shoulder down his right arm. He felt something warm and wet all over him and he saw blood and other pieces of flesh land on the picture of Jesus.

He watched as the blood dripped from the painting and mingled with that of his and his mother's. He slowly looked behind him and saw that his father had fallen in such a way that the stair railing was holding him up. Half of his father's head was missing and his right eye was bulging out of its socket.

The horrific scene would haunt his nights for many years to come. Blood and brain matter dripped from the gory wound while snot and spittle ran down his father's entire face.

The most disturbing thing about it was the smile on his father's face. He looked happier than Sean could ever remember seeing him.

"The wind shall eat up all thy pastors, and thy lovers shall go into captivity: surely then shalt thou be ashamed and confounded for all thy wickedness."

Jeremiah 22:22

2
MAY BREAK MY BONES

Albuquerque, New Mexico – Four Years Ago

The priest leaned back and stretched his six foot frame as best he could in the confined space. He ran his right hand over his forehead, brushing back some of his light blonde hair that had fallen across his field of vision. Most people considered him an attractive and athletic man, although he was more wiry than muscled.

Father Thomas Murray had been taking confession for nearly fourteen years and during that time he had heard all manner of sins being committed. During those years it seemed that everyone had committed just about every sin possible at least once in their life.

Father Murray liked confession. It was his favorite part of the job, his favorite part of a job that had become all too boring and tedious for him as of late. Everyday had turned into the same thing. Sure the people were different, but they all had the same problems, and it seemed the more he tried to be active in their spiritual lives the less he actually ended up caring.

Confession, on the other hand, was exciting. It was when he learned that everyone had a side to them they wanted to keep secret. Some members of his church even seemed to enjoy telling him their sins, as if they were excited they finally had an audience for their exploits. It was like the parable of the Pharisee and the Tax Collector come to life.

Today was particularly slow; however, and he found himself yawning more than was normal. The parade of old people coming in and confessing such ridiculous things as taking the last cup of coffee from their spouse or stealing their neighbor's paper just didn't even register on his list of things to be concerned about.

He was half asleep when the next member of his flock sat down in the confessional. The sound of the window slot sliding open startled him out of his brooding. The young woman, Laurie Alvarez, who had sat down was one of his favorite people to hear confession from and he smiled a bit as he leaned forward.

"Bless me, Father, for I have sinned. My last confession was two weeks ago," began Laurie in her low sexy voice, "In that time I have had impure thoughts of a man who is not my husband."

Father Murray was disappointed; Laurie was twenty years old and had been married just a little under a year. During that time she had cheated on her husband, who was in the military and stationed overseas, with more than nine different men and now to just hear she was having impure thoughts made him let out a small sigh. He had been hoping she would elaborate on an encounter like she did last time.

"My child, this sin is normal in those your age and in your situation," he said, "In this world, conflict often takes our loved ones far from us."

"Do you want to know who it is, Father?" she asked as she leaned closer to the window and dropped her voice low, "Do you want to know who I have been fantasizing about at night when I'm all alone?"

Father Murray's mind reeled. He licked his lips as his mind raced for some response to the question she had asked him. He found himself staring through the window slot and he felt his face flush.

Father Murray had seen her in a bikini earlier in the week when she was doing a charity car wash. He could understand why men were attracted to her. Her long, blonde hair and bright blue eyes certainly caught his attention and when you looked at her body it was not hard to imagine what she looked like under those skimpy clothes.

"I'm so tired of confessing, Father," she whispered lustily, "Wouldn't it be easier for both of us if you already knew what my sins were?"

"Wha... What are you saying?" the priest said as he felt himself becoming aroused.

"I think you know exactly what I'm saying," the young woman whispered, "I know you look at me during services. I know you stare at my body, and I know what you want."

Father Murray silently cursed himself. He had been watching her a bit too closely over the past several months, her and a few other members. Last week when he had given her communion he fantasized his manhood was in her mouth instead of the holy sacrament.

"This is a house of God. These thoughts and feelings have no place here!" Father Murray said, trying to sound angry but failing to keep the lust out of his voice.

"Oh, so you think we should take this conversation over to my house?" she playfully asked, "Or do you want to head into your chambers so you can properly give me my absolution?"

Thomas sat dumbfounded in the confessional, feeling his face flush and his lust building. There was no doubt in his mind that he wanted this woman, no doubt that he wanted to feel all the pleasure she could give him. He thought of his vows and of his future with the church, but they suddenly paled next to the intense physical feelings he was having.

He knew that it wasn't love, from what he had seen and heard from her he doubted Laurie was even capable of that emotion, and he knew there was a very real chance he would get caught. All of those thoughts only heightened his arousal and when he heard Laurie lightly panting through the window slot he knew what she was doing.

"So tell me, Father," she lowly moaned, "Do I have to keep doing this myself or are you going to help me?"

There was no defense he could muster against the urges coursing through his body. He could try to blame his weakness on the boredom that had become such a part of his daily life, or he could blame the brazen harlot that was pleasuring herself only a few short feet away from him. All in all it boiled down to one thing; Father Thomas Murray had lost his faith years ago and had just been going through the motions.

"Come to my chambers, child," he said in a low guttural voice, "There is much atoning you need to do."

Laurie had gone home a few hours ago and Thomas was still feeling the effects from their afternoon encounter. The young woman was certainly everything he had imagined her to be. Her enthusiasm and skill was something he could not describe. She had kept him occupied for the better part of three hours and there was no place in his office that they hadn't used.

He could still smell her on him and his head swam with euphoria as he remembered parts of their lovemaking... No, not lovemaking... It was animalistic fornication. The need to take, use, release and repeat had been all consuming to him.

He was roused from his musings when there was a rap on his door. He groaned as he stood up and walked toward the door in slow jerky movements, he felt like he had just hit every machine in the gym. He tucked in his shirt before opening the door and was greeted by Sister Anna Clair.

She wore her habit with dignified grace and waited patiently to be addressed. She once might have been a beautiful woman; however, her age was certainly a detriment now to her looks. Her grey eyebrows rested on top of eyes that might once have been soft, but over the years the taint of disappoint crept in and made them look hawkish and shrewd. Her aroma reminded him of the old leather bound books in his library.

"Yes, Sister?" Father Murray said.

"Father, forgive my intrusion on your meditations," the old nun's voice sounding gravelly with the strains of time, "There's a man here to see you. He said it is important and that it could not wait."

"Who is it?" asked the priest.

"It's Ryan Higgons," Sister Anna said with a faint smile on her face.

Father Murray felt a swift twinge of panic flow through him and grip him in the stomach. Ryan Higgons had been Laurie's most recent affair before him. Ryan had confessed the sin to Thomas and also had made it clear he wanted Laurie to leave her husband and marry him.

"How does he look? How is he acting?" Thomas couldn't help asking.

"He looks to have many worries, Father," she replied, "He is acting like a man who needs guidance."

The panic in Thomas slowly began spreading to his chest. If Sister Anna knew any more than she was letting on she hid it well. The old nun had seen many things in her life and he doubted he was the first priest to ever have sex in these chambers. Father Murray had the sudden urge to shake the old woman until she spilled everything to him. He had to know what was going through her head.

"Is there anything else, Sister?" he asked with a slight hint of anger in his voice.

"No, Father," she replied with the smile still on her face.

"Then send him in," he commanded then shut his door.

Sister Anna gave a nod to the closed door and returned to the receiving area where Ryan waited. The old nun had indeed heard Thomas and the harlot engaging in their appetites. She didn't care much about the young lady, but she was very disappointed in the priest. As she entered the waiting room she felt a momentary twinge of pity for the young man seated in one of the many red velvety chairs.

The man was just a little younger than Father Murray, more physically fit and a few inches taller. He had black hair that was disheveled and his brown eyes were red from crying and seemed hollow to her. Sister Anna had overheard some of the distasteful discussions this man had with the harlot and hardened her heart as his attention focused on her.

He stood up when she entered the room and stuffed his hands deep into his pants pockets. Sister Anna noted his shoes and pants were dirty, as if he just came from his landscaping job.

"Father Murray is in his chambers. He said you may enter." After delivering the message, the old nun returned to the kitchen to finish her cleaning duties.

Ryan walked down the hall to Father Murray's door. He had been here a few times over the past three years for advice on important matters in his life. Today he would be asking questions he never thought he would need to.

When Ryan knocked on the door he heard movement from inside. After a short wait the door opened and in front of him stood Father Murray. He was dressed in his robes and motioned him to come in with a smile on his face.

"Ryan, it's good to see you," Thomas said trying to sound cheerful, "What can I do for you?"

Ryan entered the room and sat down on one of the plush chairs in front of Thomas's desk. His hands were still in his pockets and he stared vacantly ahead. The priest locked the door then walked around his desk and sat in his chair. Ryan looked at him for few seconds and then began to cry.

Thomas was at a loss for words. If it had been any other member of his congregation, or if he hadn't indulged in his earlier activities, he would have walked around and hugged the man. As it was, Father Murray was feeling very uneasy in his presence.

"Father, I need your help," sobbed Ryan.

"What is it, my son? I am here for... The church is here for anything you need," Thomas corrected himself.

"It's Laurie, Father," Ryan continued to sob, "She... She told me earlier she didn't want to see me anymore."

Father Murray leaned back in his chair. So Laurie had broken it off with him. Thomas thought about the implications of that. Did it mean that he now had her full attention? The thought made him uneasy and excited at the same time. Looking at Ryan, he suddenly felt disgusted with the man.

Why was he crying his eyes out over a woman he never should have become involved with, let alone attached to, in the first place? Ryan surely should have known that the situation was not going to end in his favor.

"Ryan, Laurie is a married woman. She made sacred vows to her husband, vows that you were directly involved in breaking with her," Thomas felt like a hypocrite when he first started speaking, but then the feeling changed over to one of superiority.

"Who are you to cry when it is you who have caused such heartache to come to that family? How do you justify your feelings when you know there never should have been anything between you at all? It's not love you're feeling, it is guilt!"

Ryan sobbed even harder as Thomas spoke harshly to him. He was hurting enough as it was and to hear the truth being spoken so coldly, as well as the unspoken truth, caused even more pain to stab through his heart.

"Father," he blubbered, "I have done something horrible!"

The next round of verbal bashing died in Father Murray's throat before he could utter it. He felt a chill run down his spine and settle in his toes. He looked at Ryan and clamped his mouth shut. The man was staring at him through his tears and his jaw was set with determination. Thomas slowly started pushing his chair away from the desk that separated him and Ryan.

"Father," began Ryan as he fought against his emotions for control of his voice, "I thought you were a good man; a man that was dedicated to helping others weaker than him; a man who understood that some things were sacred."

Ryan's voice became clearer and gained strength as he spoke. The tears, though still slowly and steadily falling from his eyes, started to draw less attention from Father Murray. Now, Thomas was overtaken completely by the emotion pouring from Ryan's soul.

"I know it was wrong," Ryan suddenly roared from the chair. His eyes narrowing as he stared at the priest who had fallen back into his chair at the outburst.

"It was all wrong, but I loved her! I loved her so much!" Ryan wailed as he jumped to his feet and leaned toward Thomas.

The priest slowly stood up and took a deep breath. Ryan had started to drool during his tirade and the saliva was mixing with snot that had been hanging from his chin from all the weeping. Looking at the disgusting concoction made Thomas's stomach feel sick, a feeling that was pale compared to the fear that was rising sharply in him.

"Did you love her, too?!" Ryan demanded of the stunned priest.

"I... I... What do you mean 'DID' I love her'?" stammered the priest.

Ryan's growing fury exploded in the form of a left cross that connected squarely with the priest's jaw.

Thomas didn't see the punch that knocked him over the arm of chair. One moment he was on his feet and the next he was looking up at Ryan from the floor behind his desk. His nose crushed and splayed under his left eye.

"Unnnnhhhhh!" Father Murray groaned in shock as he tried to bring himself to a sitting position.

He could see Ryan slowly walking around the desk toward him through eyes that were fast watering up. He tried getting to his feet but was dizzy from the blow. Blood was flowing from his ruined nose and soaking into his clothes; he could taste more of it in his mouth and felt it in the back of his throat.

"Did you love her!?" Ryan screamed as he drug the priest to his feet by the front of his robe.

The sudden movements made Thomas feel faint and he felt like he was going to throw up. Ryan was gripping him so tight his skin was being pinched underneath his robe and shirt. Father Murray blinked several times trying to clear his vision and he felt a wave of nausea and then a moment of embarrassment when he vomited on the front of Ryan's shirt. Ryan seemed not to notice.

Ryan smelled blood on the man in front of him. The look in the priest's eyes was one of terror. The smells and look reminded him of what happened earlier and Ryan started shaking Father Murray like a ragdoll. Ryan also started wailing like a child who had dropped his favorite toy just out of reach.

Thomas's senses were reeling. His eyes were clearing up but his legs felt like rubber. If it wasn't for the painful way Ryan was holding him up, he realized he would have already fallen over again. When the crazed man started shaking him more things came into focus.

"Leh' me go!" the priest screamed through his pain, his speech slurred.

Ryan gave no indication he heard Thomas, if indeed he had heard him at all, and continued to shake him. Thomas brought his knee up as hard as he could into his assailant's groin.

Ryan grunted and shoved Father Murray as hard as he could against the desk. The priest hit his back hard against it and twisted painfully over the heavy oak, comically landing in his chair for a brief moment before his momentum carried him over and onto the floor again.

"She was just a fuck to you!" the priest heard Ryan growl.

There was a deep burning pain in his back as Thomas got to his feet. His legs were still a bit shaky but he had them under control. He wasn't surprised to see that Ryan had moved between him and the door. He was surprised to see that Ryan was holding the silver letter opener that he kept on his desk.

"What do you want from me?!" screamed Thomas.

Ryan's face lost all sense of any composure as tears started rolling from his eyes again. His whole body seemed to convulse with sobs, and he kept wiping his eyes with his sleeve while making low moaning sounds like a wounded animal, never losing his stare on the priest.

"She told me about you," the shaking man said. "She told me she was fucking you and that she didn't want me anymore. She said she was tired of me."

Father Murray froze. Even though he had already figured out the reason for the attack he couldn't actually believe that Laurie had been so stupid! What kind of perverted thrill did she get from telling this psychotic a story like that? It didn't make any sense to Thomas.

"I told her I forgave her and that I would try to be more of what she wanted," Ryan said.

The priest watched as the man tried to regain control of himself. Each time it seemed he was getting close, another shaking fit would hit Ryan and the movements bordered on a seizure.

"Do you know what she did?" the man said between clattering teeth, "She laughed at me!"

Ryan made a lunge at Thomas, the letter opener leading the way. Father Murray shuffled to his left and leaned slightly back, the edge of the opener skipped across his ribs and he felt a brief flash of pain. Ryan's movement carried him in front of Father Murray and the priest made a wild swing at the larger man with his right arm.

By some miracle the blow connected and Ryan went down to one knee. Thomas swung a left hook and caught him just under the jaw. Ryan was knocked to the ground and the priest bolted for the door.

He was fumbling with the deadbolt when Ryan grabbed his head from behind and slammed his face into the door. More pain than he ever thought possible screamed at him from his nose and he felt himself being hurled to the ground.

He got to his knees just in time to catch Ryan's boot on the side of his head. He fell backwards from the force of the blow and stared numbly up at the ceiling trying to force his arms and legs to obey his will.

"I didn't know what to do!" wailed Ryan, his voice sounding very far away.

"She just kept laughing at me and I just wanted her to stop. I just wanted her to listen to me. I just wanted to explain how much she meant to me, and I would do anything for her!"

Father Murray saw Ryan above him and tried to roll away. He was helped along in that endeavor by a series of kicks from the crazed man. With each strike the priest felt more strength leaving his body.

"When I hit her she stopped laughing," Ryan whispered suddenly, stopping his flurry of kicks.

Thomas tried to understand the implications of what Ryan was saying, but the pain and fear in him made it hard. The priest rolled over onto his hands and knees and was startled to see the amount of blood that was falling from him. *No wonder I feel so damn weak,* he thought. Ryan's voice brought his attention back to what was happening.

"She started to scream so I hit her again. I kept hitting her until she was quiet. When I saw her like that... When I saw what I did... She was, just all quiet you know? She was so quiet but she kept staring at me. Blood was everywhere. She had stopped moving and laughing and she was just so quiet and so still. So quiet and still. She just kept staring at me you know?"

Father Murray dared a glance up at his attacker. Ryan had his back to him and was looking out the window. Outside there was flashing red and blue lights and Thomas felt immense relief flood through him. Sister Anna must have called the police when she heard the screaming.

Thomas tried to get to his feet, but he was too weak from the fight and loss of blood. Ryan must have heard him moving because he looked down at him. Thomas felt his arms give out and he collapsed on the carpet face down.

They both heard a pounding on the door a few moments later. Thomas started crawling toward the sound as best he could. He looked up at Ryan, who was just staring down at him with tears streaming down his face.

"I killed her, Father!" Ryan wailed, "I loved her, but I killed her!"

"Open the door! Police!" shouts came from out in the hall as the pounding on the door grew louder.

"I'm..." began Thomas, "I'm so sorry for all of this."

Father Murray continued to crawl toward the door. Ryan slowly walked alongside him, switching the letter opener from hand to hand. Thomas knew the man was going to kill him, he just didn't know when Ryan would work up to it. He did know that it would take a while before the police could get through the heavy oaken door with the deadbolt.

Thomas gathered all of his remaining strength and swung his right foot toward the back of Ryan's legs. When his foot landed just behind Ryan's left leg, the man tumbled down on top of him.

In a flurry of punches and shoves the letter opener somehow found its way into Father Murray's grasp blade first. Thomas felt the edge cut deep into his hand while at the same time he felt Ryan's meaty fist strike him in the back of the head and his vision instantly became blurry.

He got his left hand around the handle and began slashing wildly at Ryan. He managed to get into a sitting position while he slashed back and forth. Occasionally he would feel the blade of the opener hit Ryan, sometimes stabbing but most of the time cutting into his attacker.

All the while he could hear voices yelling out in the hall and then a much louder banging on the door, like a sledgehammer hitting it. The blurry form of Ryan was laying a few feet from him and was softly moaning. Father Murray stabbed him a few more times and each blow was met with a soft wet gurgling sound.

Thomas felt the opener slip from his hand. He no longer had the strength to grip it. He fell to the carpet meaning to just rest for a little bit. He could feel himself losing consciousness but held on until the police busted through the door.

Father Thomas Murray was taken to the hospital with several lacerations, a bruised kidney, a broken nose, four broken ribs and detached retinas. Ryan Higgons died en route to the medical facility from the multiple stab wounds he received during the fight.

The body of Laurie Alvarez was found in her apartment later that evening by police. When Father Murray was interviewed about the attack, he told police that Ryan had came to him for advice after committing the murder. Thomas lied and told police that he was attacked when he tried to convince Ryan to give himself up.

Sister Anna told police that Ryan Higgons had visited Father Murray on several occasions when he had a spiritual crisis and always seemed much better after talking to the Father. She also told police that she had called them because she thought someone was breaking into the church because of all the loud noises.

Thomas didn't know how much truth was in Sister Anna's story, but by the way she would always smile smugly at him when they were alone, he had a good idea of how much she really knew.

Three months later he requested and was granted a transfer from his superiors. Sister Anna smiled as he got into his cab and rode away from the church for the last time. She thought he was being transferred to some little town in Missouri, but didn't care much. She was just happy he was gone.

THE APOCALYPSE OF ENOCH

"But I say unto you, Love your enemies, bless them that curse you, do good to them that hate you, and pray for them who despitefully use you, and persecute you; that you may be children of your Father in heaven. He causes his sun to rise on the evil and the good, and sends rain on the righteous and the unrighteous."

Matthew 5:44-45

3
THE HORN ON THE BUS GOES BEEP BEEP BEEP

Owensville, Missouri – Two Years Ago

Sean gazed through the window of the minivan and let out a small sigh, his breath causing the cold glass to fog up. He was happy that Miss Fritte offered him the front seat, even though it meant riding next to an asshole.

He looked over at the pudgy older man who was driving and then quickly wiped the fog away before Mister Dabner noticed what he was doing. Sean dared a glance at the backseat and felt a little better when Miss Fritte gave him a wink and a knowing smile. Sean returned the smile for a moment and then faced toward the window again.

"How much longer will the drive be?" he asked, not looking away from the scenery as it rolled passed.

Jake Dabner glanced in the rearview mirror long enough to make eye contact with Judy Fritte. The younger woman shook her head and had a worried look on her face. Jake made a snorting sound then looked back at the road.

"You don't sound too excited," said the kindly woman.

"That's because I'm not."

"Not a good attitude to have," Judy playfully scolded.

"Jesus f'in' Christ, Sean," Jake chimed in, "Do you have any idea how much work Miss Fritte has put in trying to place your sorry ass!?"

"Jake, don't start!" Judy snapped, "Things have been rough for him!"

"Oh hell Judy, things have been rough on everybody!" barked Jake.

Sean stared out the window as the argument got louder. He watched as the world sped past him, remembering similar trips in the past. Sean put his head against the cool window and felt the jostle of each bump on the road; it was very relaxing and made him tired. He closed his eyes and secretly hoped that this trip would be different.

"...don't you think Sean?" Judy's use of his name snapped him back from the edge of sleep.

"Uh-huh," the boy said while yawning, not having any clue what he had just agreed with.

"I hope so because I'm getting tired of hauling you back and forth all the time," the fat man mumbled under his breath just loud enough for Sean to hear.

Sean ran his hands through his hair and stretched, ignoring Mister Dabner's taunt. It seemed like they had been driving for hours since they left the children's home in St. Louis.

"At least Owensville is a smaller town. They have almost no crime there," Miss Fritte said.

"Great that means everyone will know who the new orphan boy is."

He regretted the words as soon as he said them. He looked back at Miss Fritte and saw true care and compassion in her eyes for him. Sean knew the lady had tried everything she could to get him adopted the past six years and that she felt horrible that things always seemed to fall through at the last minute.

"I'm sorry, Miss Fritte," the boy said looking over his right shoulder at her, "I appreciate this, I really do."

"You better..." began Jake.

"You're welcome, Sean!" Judy interrupted, "I know you will do great here."

"I still don't understand what the Catholic Church is trying to prove here," Jake said towards Judy, "What kind of social experiment is this again? You take orphans from city facilities and place them in churches so they can be unpaid workers?"

"No, it's nothing like that!" she said, tired of trying to explain it to him.

"They live as a ward of the priest. They go to public school and can be as active in extracurricular activities as they want to be. They work ten hours a week as directed by their guardian and must attend all services."

"When participants in the program turn eighteen they can go to college and the church will cover all expenses for the first two years. After that it is based on their academics."

"What if I don't want to go to college?" asked Sean.

"In that case you'll need to find a job, kid!" Jake snapped at him.

Sean felt a moment of hate rise up in him towards the fat prick. He wanted to lash out but instead he bit the inside of his lower lip and returned to staring out the window. His temper always got the better of him and was one of the biggest reasons he could never find a permanent home.

"You're a smart kid. You need to go to college," Judy admonished him.

The boy looked back at her and gave another brief smile, something seemed off about it but Judy thought it might just be his nerves. Making Sean smile was a mission for her daily. This morning since they had left she had counted three of them, a new record.

St. Louis was far behind them and Sean was taking in all the open space along Highway 50. He had not been this far out in the country since that trip to a farm just outside of Washington. Sean had let himself forget the peaceful feeling he had while there, he knew peace never lasted.

"We're almost there, Judy," Mister Dabner said, "Damn this is a long ass drive!"

"Jake, language please!" scolded Miss Fritte.

"Awww hell, you have yer' head in the sand if ya' think these kids don't cuss," quipped Jake.

"Why can't you be nice to her!" Sean suddenly yelled,

finally losing his temper.

The boy clenched his hands into fists and started banging on the dash of the vehicle. Mister Dabner glared at the boy and raised his arm as if to strike him. Sean stared back at him, daring the fat man to carry out his threat with the look he gave him.

"Stop it! Both of you!" yelled Judy.

"This little bastard needs to learn some respec'!" growled Jake, his eyes switching back and forth between the road and the child next to him.

"You need to learn it you fat fuck!" Sean yelled back at him.

Jake's eyes went wide and he gripped the steering wheel so tight his knuckles turned white. Sean continued to stare at Jake and each time the fat man looked over at him the boy's look became more hate filled.

Judy sat in the backseat feeling completely at a loss. She knew that Sean and Jake didn't like each other. Her stomach had actually turned when she saw that Mister Dabner was the assigned driver for the day. She had thought that there might be some kind of altercation but didn't expect such venom.

She reached out and gently rubbed Sean's shoulder trying to calm him down. The boy was shaking with barely contained fury.

"Sean, try to let it go. There are people like him all over the world and you're going to have to learn to deal with them in a different way," she said.

"What are you say—" began Jake.

"She's saying you're a mean person that likes to hurt people. You're a bully, Jake, and I don't like you very much," Sean said.

The boy had come a long way over the years at getting his emotions under control and Judy could feel him stop shaking after he spoke. The calm and matter of fact tone in his voice was something to be commended. It was as if he was nonchalantly chatting about the sun outside.

"I think you—" Jake started.

"I think YOU need to just drive, Mister Dabner!" Judy interrupted, "There've already been complaints against you and I'll be making another when we get back. Don't say or do anything stupid for the rest of the trip and maybe mine won't be as bad as some I've read!"

Jake sputtered for a few seconds and then made some huffing noises. He kept his eyes focused on the road and the van was quiet for a few minutes before Sean spoke.

"I'm sorry, Miss Fritte. I didn't mean to upset you," the orphan said as he looked back at her.

"It's okay, buddy. Just try to remember that getting mad doesn't help anything. All it does is make it hard to think clearly. People do and say things they don't mean when they're mad," she replied.

The image of his father's death grin came to him and he shuddered. It wasn't hard for Sean to imagine how much anger and rage his dad felt. Sometimes, when he got mad, he just wanted everyone around him hurt. Even the good people like Miss Fritte.

After he had a chance to calm down he always felt bad about wanting that, but it never stopped the thought from entering his mind the next time he got pissed.

The sign for the junction of Highway 28 caught Sean's attention. He remembered Highway 28 had something to do with the town he was being taken to. As Sean was trying to remember, the van hit an uneven patch of asphalt and lurched to the left. Jake quickly recovered control of the vehicle and slowed down.

The fat man swore under his breath as he turned onto the new road and slowly built up speed. Miss Fritte leaned forward and gently put her hand on Sean's arm. The boy looked back at her and she squeezed his elbow, leaning in even closer so she could whisper.

"Don't let anyone like Jake Dabner make you feel like you're not important. Don't let them push you into doing something you'll regret later. People like that aren't worth it," she quietly said and then sat back in her seat.

Sean watched her retreat and then he looked over at Jake. It was almost as if he could see right into his heart. When Sean looked at him now, all he saw was someone who was scared and bitter about his own life.

Jake saw the boy eying him out of the corner of his vision

and turned toward him with angry words on the tip of his tongue. He choked on them when he saw the look Sean had on his face. Pity was something Jake was not use to seeing.

Jake glared at the boy and mouthed "fuck you" to him. Sean turned away from him and watched the passing countryside again. After a few moments the orphan leaned his head against the window and let the motion of the vehicle carry him off to sleep.

Miss Fritte gently shook Sean as they pulled into the parking lot of the church in Owensville, Missouri. The boy stirred a bit but continued to sleep.

Mister Dabner turned off the van and looked at the bothersome kid seated next to him. A wicked grin flashed across the older man's face and he held down the horn for a few seconds.

Jake felt a rush of twisted pleasure as he watched Sean's eyes open wide with terror at the loud wail of the horn. The sadistic man chuckled when the boy started screaming and thrashing around.

"Damn it, Jake!" yelled Judy as she tried to calm the frightened child.

"It was only a joke, damn!" the fat man responded.

"You fucker!" yelled Sean.

"That's it kid, let the priest hear your potty mouth," laughed Jake.

The fat man kept laughing as Sean fought to regain his composure. Judy hugged the boy as hard as she could from the backseat. On instinct she reached down and held onto Sean's wrists, preventing him at the last second from lashing out physically at Jake.

Mister Dabner reached down and unbuckled his seatbelt while opening the door to the van. His laughter turned to a wheeze as he stepped out of the driver's seat onto the hard asphalt of the parking lot.

He looked inside through a side window as he stiffly shuffled to the back of the van. He rolled his eyes when he saw Judy whispering something into the kid's ear. Didn't she understand that the little freak was a hopeless case?

Jake leaned against the rear door of the van and pulled out a pack of cigarettes. Putting one in his mouth, he inhaled deeply as he lit it. He watched Judy continue hugging and talking to Sean for a few minutes while he smoked.

The fat man threw his half-finished cigarette down and ground it out under the toe of his right boot. He opened the back of the van and grabbed one of the kid's suitcases, grunting under the weight of it as he set it down next to him.

"Come on kid," he said as he reached for the next piece of luggage, "I'm not your personal fuckin' valet here. Move your ass!"

Sean flashed him a smile and slowly stepped out of the vehicle. Judy glared at him for a moment before opening her door and stepping out. Jake chuckled under his breath. Let the stupid bitch think filing a report would matter. He had too much dirt on the boss for him to get fired for anything short of murder.

Jake was about to yell at the kid again when he felt a firm hand on his right shoulder.

"Aww shit!" the fat man yelled. Jake jumped with fright and plunged headfirst into the back of the van.

He landed on his stomach and the wind was knocked from his lungs. Jake rolled over onto his back in a panic to see who had grabbed him. The sun hid the features of the figure standing in front of him. The fat man raised his arms up to try to block the glare and his heart beat faster when he felt two strong hands close over his wrists.

"Dem' words ain't nice ta' say," said a slow voice.

"I... I... Let me GO!" yelled Jake.

Sean and Judy came around to the back of the van and saw a heavily muscled middle-aged man in dirty grey overhauls holding Mister Dabner's arms. The man had a sad look on his boyish face as he looked down at his captive.

Jake kicked the man a few times. Judy winced in sympathetic pain as she saw two solid blows land in the stranger's crotch. The muscled man showed no reaction at all to Jake's struggles.

THE APOCALYPSE OF ENOCH

Sean watched in fascination as the man lifted Jake into a standing position. Sweat was pouring down the fat man's face from his struggles and his breathing was labored. It looked to Sean like Mister Dabner might have a heart attack at any moment.

"Apologize ta' da' boy and purdy lady," the stranger said slowly.

Jake stood dumfounded and stared into the man's bright blue eyes. His chest felt like it was on fire and he was gasping for air. He tried to pull his arms away several times and didn't so much as cause the strong man to even sway on his feet.

"Fer' da' words," the overhaul wearing man said, "Da' words ya' said ta' da' boy in front uh da' purdy lady."

Jake tried falling backwards into the van. He leaned back as best he could and tried to push with his legs. He was amazed as his three hundred and fifty four pound body was pulled back into an upright position by the stranger.

"Apologize... Fer' da' words."

Jake was at the end of his rope. He had never been manhandled like this before and he felt completely helpless. He started shaking from fear and fought back tears. The fat man tried to apologize but all that came out was a hacking sound and some sobbing noises.

Judy and Sean stood transfixed by the scene before them. Both of them had different thoughts in their minds. Judy, horrified at the thought of what might happen next, had grabbed Sean and was hugging him close to her. She feared that at any moment the large man would turn more violent.

Sean, on the other hand, silently willed the stranger to carry out Miss Fritte's unspoken fears. He wanted Jake's fat ass hurt, beaten and bleeding. Sean found himself smiling when he looked at the fear clearly painted on his tormentor's face.

"Michael, drop him!" commanded a new voice from behind them.

As soon as the last word was uttered the muscled man let Jake go. The fat man instantly fell heavily on his ass in the back of the van. Jake tried to stand but his legs were shaking so much from fear that it was impossible.

All heads turned to the man who had spoken. A young

priest stood with his arms crossed in front of his chest and a sour expression on his face. A day's growth of beard was on the man's handsome face, giving him a rugged look that Judy found intriguing.

"He used bad words," Michael said slowly, "In front of da' purdy lady and da' boy."

"I know he did," said the priest. His expression softened as he spoke, "That will be all for today, Michael. I will see you tomorrow."

"K' Fadder'," Michael said, walking away like nothing had happened.

"Father Murray?" asked Judy.

"Yes and you must be Judy Fritte," the priest said as he walked over and shook her hand.

Mister Dabner had finally managed to stand up and was looking sheepishly at the group. Sean glanced at him and gave a cocky smile. The fat man did not have the energy to make any response.

"Please accept my apologies for Michael. He is a bit slower than most but there is a very kind heart in that huge chest of his."

"You could of fooled me!" grumbled Jake.

"Michael has… Strong opinions on how women and children should be treated. I don't think he would have seriously injured you, but it would have been best to just apologize for whatever you had done and not antagonized him further."

"Are you fucking serious?" asked Jake.

Thomas stared at him for a second before responding, "I think it best if you were to wait in the van."

"Fuck that!" yelled Jake, "I'm gonna' press charges against that fucking retard!"

Father Murray shook his head slowly back and forth then let out a sigh. "You must not be a fast learner my friend," he said while pointing in the direction Michael had walked.

As if on cue, Michael peaked around the corner of the church.

"Oh Fuck ME!" Mister Dabner yelled as he scurried into the driver's seat through the rear of the van.

He cranked the ignition and when the engine started the fat man gunned the vehicle out of the parking lot, the back doors swinging wildly as he careened around a corner and sped up

Main Street. Michael had watched him drive away and then disappeared around the side of the church again.

Sean laughed at the sight. He laughed until his sides hurt and tears were rolling down his cheeks. The boy laughed even louder when Miss Fritte joined in. Sean was wiping his arm across his face when he finally got a good look at the priest who he would be living with for the next six years.

Father Thomas Murray was looking at Miss Fritte with an odd expression. It reminded Sean of how some of the kids at the orphanage looked at potential parents when they came to visit. It was almost like a hunger.

Sean felt a chill run down his spine and he shuddered. When he looked back up he saw the priest looking at him. The odd, hungry look had been replaced with one of... Indifference?

"Young man, I am Father Thomas Murray." The priest said, "You can call me Father Murray."

"Yes, Father Murray."

"Don't sound so down," the priest said while smiling, "It can be a lot of fun around here."

Thomas looked at Miss Fritte as he finished his sentence then continued, "So should we call your boss and tell him you were stranded here or would you like to make other arrangements to get back home?"

Judy blushed under the gaze of the handsome priest and smiled back at him, "I guess other arrangements can be made."

She instantly felt like a fool. Flirting with a priest... What was she thinking? When she looked up at him to make some small talk her breath caught in her chest. Father Murray had looked her up and down a few times, and blatantly so! He must have wanted her to see him do it.

Judy felt her face flush and she was a little embarrassed. She looked at Sean. The boy was silently watching the exchange between them. Judy had learned long ago that Sean was a very bright child that picked up on subtlety a lot more instinctively than most adults. She briefly wondered what he was thinking, but stopped when the priest touched her arm.

"I have some business to take care of in Union tomorrow," he said while slowly moving his hand down her arm until he lightly held her hand in his, "It would be no trouble for me to drive a little further. Of course that would mean you would have to stay the night here."

Miss Fritte felt her face flush even more as she looked into Father Thomas's eyes. There was something in them, something mischievous and playful, which made her instantly attracted to the man.

Father Murray smiled gently at her and let go of her hand. He turned and lifted one of Sean's suitcases with far greater ease than Mister Dabner had managed. The boy looked at him for a moment then hurriedly picked up his remaining piece of luggage.

"If you both would care to follow me we can get things squared away for the evening," said the priest as he walked toward the church.

The orphan walked after the priest, the heavy suitcase causing him to sway awkwardly. Judy followed Sean, but her eyes did not leave the priest's body as she moved towards the church.

"I think you're gonna' like it here, Sean."

Sean glanced back at her and stopped himself from nodding when he noticed how intently she was looking at the priest. Sean felt a moment of jealousy wash over him but quickly suppressed it before it turned into rage.

This guy was a priest. There was no way anything would happen between Miss Fritte and him! The orphan allowed a few moments of muffled laughter for himself before he followed Father Murray into the church.

Thomas lay on his back and watched Judy sleeping peacefully next to him. He allowed a smile to creep onto his face as he carefully got out of his bed and made his way to the bathroom. He thought about the evening's events as he relieved himself.

After showing the kid to his room he had taken both of them out to dinner. Once back at his house next to the church they had all watched *Star Wars* and then he and Judy put Sean to bed.

Seducing the lady had been easy after that. Yes, he thought him and the boy would get along great. Yes, he would look after him like he was his own. Yes, he always wanted kids but being a priest...

Judy had been a very willing partner. Almost more so than the young foreign student he was currently involved with. Jacqueline was a sophomore at the University of Missouri in Rolla and she was anxious to experience all of America, including the decadence.

Father Murray lay back down next to her and looked at her naked body. He had a brief fantasy about introducing the two women to see where things would go but quickly dismissed the idea. Most likely Miss Fritte would wake up and, once she was thinking more clearly, would hate herself for what happened earlier.

The fallen priest closed his eyes and slowly drifted off to sleep. His last conscious thoughts were of the uncomfortable drive he would have to make in the morning to take Judy back to St. Louis.

Children of Enoch: Dark Harvest is available on Amazon.com and from New Babel Books. The second book in the series, The Reaping of Sorrows, will be out Fall 2015.

CHARACTERS

Ami Taylor- Wife of Daniel Emery Taylor.
April Simpson- Reporter/Anchor for FOX2 in Saint Louis. www.facebook.com/AprilSimpsonTV
Arianna Lamb- Damsels of Dorkington member.
Artez Hardin- Saint Louis Police Officer.
Benisha Abe- American living in Japan, home for a visit.
Billy Tackett- Top horror artist in America. www.BillyTackett.com
Blythe Renay- Damsel of Dorkington member.
Chloe-AKA-Adrastea (Latin for inescapable)- little girl brought into room 425 in Maryville. First child to be taken in the Rapture.
Corey Phillips- CEO of Black Pigeon Press and owner of "Gameday." www.blackpigeonpress.com
The Damsels of Dorkington –Group of entertainers famous for their skits and comedy on the convention circuit. www.DamselsofDorkington.com
Dani Burke- Woman that comes in and lies down next to Frank Fradella right before the 4th seal is opened.
Daniel Emery Taylor- Actor from Road Trip and

Return of the Swamp Thing. danielemerytaylor.com

Danielle Nevin- A nurse at Anderson Hospital and last person to be Raptured.

David Dyer- Owner of St Louis Science Fiction/Fantasy convention named "CON-tamination."
www.Con-Tamination.com

Dean "Midas" Maynard- X-factor TV personality caught in the Apocalypse in Memphis.
www.deanmidasmaynard.com

Doctor Josh Poos- Doctor working with the CDC on the Abaddon Virus.

Frank Fradella- Old man in Anderson Hospital that is visited by an angel and given the power of the coming Rapture.

Hometown Comics- Comic Store located at 110 East Vandilia,
Edwardsville IL 62025 www.hometowncomics.com

Irma Cassorla- A CNA at Anderson Hospital in Maryville, IL.

Jeff Yenzer- Damsels of Dorkington member.

Jim O'Rear- Actor trapped at Con-tamination in Saint Louis. www.jimorear.com

Kirby Krackle- Awesome band with many genre songs. www.KirbyKracklemusic.com

Matt Hill- Actor (Raphael from Teenage Mutant Ninja Turtles). www.Matt-hill.com

Pete Koch- Former Oakland Raider and Heartbreak Ridge actor. www.PeteKoch.com

Peter and Angie Mayhew- Peter played Chewbacca in every Star Wars film. www.PeterMayhew.com

Private Shane Nettleton- A man awaiting military trial for killing a captured insurgent that tortured and killed a civilian by cutting his head off on video. Shane has been relocated to a reserve unit and is out on bond, put up by his unit and internet fans.

Randy Roach- High School graduate on his way to the science fiction and fantasy convention in Saint Louis named Con-tamination.

Rebecca Hultz- Shane Nettleton's girlfriend.

Ryan Roach- Former EMT and church musician on his

way to the science fiction and fantasy convention in Saint Louis named Con-tamination.

Sara Delp- School Teacher at Troy Middle School.

Sheree Speckman- Lab tech working with Doctor Poos.

Sinjin Oleszczuk- Z.O.D. member of the Double'O First Cosplayer. Runs CCG website for advanced looks at MMOs for their subscribers.

Stephanie Schofield- Z.O.D. member of the Double'O First cosplayer.

Steven Tibbs- Professional rapper and Biz Markie collaborator. www.StevenTibbs.com

Terry Naughton-Disney animator and Abyss Walker Artist. www.TerryNaughton.com

Tori Bilderback- Stranded in Memphis, TN while on vacation.

Z.O.D. (Zombification, Orientation, and Defense)- A nationwide cosplay group dedicated to edifying the public on how to survive a Zombie Apocalypse.

About the Author

Shane Moore grew up on a farm in rural Illinois. An only child that was six miles from his nearest peer, Shane often created wild tales of heroes and villains during his many trips into the deep woods that surrounded his rural home.

Shane was accelerated in his class and started his senior year of high school at age sixteen. After graduating and getting a waiver for his age, Shane joined the United States Navy to pay for college. He participated in campaigns; "Provide Hope" and "Secure Democracy" during the Yugoslavian civil war. Shane received several naval awards and citations and was one of the highest trained members of his ship.

After getting out of the service, Shane began college. He was soon hired by the Carlinville Police Department, beginning his multiple venue police career. Shane retired as a detective for the Gillespie Police Department after serving twelve years. His police career was quite notable with awards for bravery and with one life saving medal. He was named Officer of the Year in 2005.

A lesser known truth about Shane is that he played eight years of semi pro football with the Central Illinois Cougars. Shane is the team's all-time tackle leader and holds the record for most special teams tackles in a season and the most tackles in a game. Shane received many awards including Defensive Player of the Year in 2005.

On January 14th, 2008 Shane retired from his police career to be a professional novelist.

Mr. Moore resides in Central Illinois with his son, Dakota.

Check out these other great titles from New Babel Books:

Abyss Walker titles

Core Series
"The Plea of Apollisian"
"The Trial of Innocence"
"Darrion-Quieness"
"Death of Kings"
"Tides of Winter"
"Return of the Father"

The Wererat's Tale Series
"The Wererat's Tale-Of Rats and Men"
"The Wererat's Tale-Ring of the Nonul"
"The Wererat's Tale-The Collar of Perdition"

White Wraith Series
"White Wraith-The Escape"
"White Wraith-Lock of Requ"
"White Wraith-Malestrom Serpents"

For additional NBB titles, visit: www.newbabelbooks.com

THE APOCALYPSE OF ENOCH

Go to www.Zod001.com and Join for Free!

SHANE MOORE

Peter Mayhew

Matt Hill

Daniel Emery Taylor

THE APOCALYPSE OF ENOCH

Jim O'Rear

Steve Tibbs

April Simpson

SHANE MOORE

Terry Naughton

Billy Tackett

Pete Koch

THE APOCALYPSE OF ENOCH

SHANE MOORE

Made in the USA
Lexington, KY
02 September 2017